August von Kotzebue, Anne Plumptre, Thomas Dutton

The Natural Son

A Play in Five Acts

August von Kotzebue, Anne Plumptre, Thomas Dutton

The Natural Son
A Play in Five Acts

ISBN/EAN: 9783337397449

Printed in Europe, USA, Canada, Australia, Japan

Cover: Foto ©Andreas Hilbeck / pixelio.de

More available books at **www.hansebooks.com**

THE NATURAL SON;

A PLAY,

IN FIVE ACTS,

BY

AUGUSTUS VON KOTZEBUE,

Poet Laureat and Director of the Imperial Theatre at Vienna.

BEING THE ORIGINAL OF

LOVERS' VOWS,

NOW PERFORMING, WITH UNIVERSAL APPLAUSE, AT THE

THEATRE ROYAL, COVENT GARDEN.

TRANSLATED FROM THE GERMAN

By ANNE PLUMPTRE,

AUTHOR OF THE RECTOR'S SON, ANTOINETTE, &c.

Who has prefixed

A PREFACE,

Explaining the Alterations in the Representation; and

A LIFE OF KOTZEBUE.

FOURTH EDITION. REVISED.

LONDON:

PRINTED FOR R. PHILLIPS:

SOLD BY H. D. SYMONDS, PATER-NOSTER-ROW; CARPENTER AND CO. OLD BOND STREET; R. H. WESTLY, STRAND; AND BY ALL OTHER BOOKSELLERS

1798.

Tranſlator's Preface.

THE flattering Reception which the Natural Son, under the adopted Title of LOVERS' VOWS, has experienced from an Engliſh Audience, in an abridged and altered State, affords Reaſon to believe that a complete Tranſlation of ſo admirable a Drama will obtain at leaſt an equal Degree of Public Approbation. This Drama, ſince its firſt Appearance in Germany, has uniformly ranked among the moſt favourite Productions of the Pen of its illuſtrious Author; its Celebrity had long attracted the Notice of the Tranſlator, and a Peruſal of it ſatisfied her, that it was one of thoſe brilliant Dramatic Meteors, whoſe Luſtre ought to be extended from the German to the Engliſh Horizon.

Her original Deſign was to adapt it to the London Stage, and with this View ſhe actually proceeded in the Tranſlation; when, however, ſhe had made conſiderable Progreſs, ſhe learnt that her Deſign had been already anticipated, and that a Tranſlation, by a foreign Gentleman, had been placed in the Hands of Mrs. Inchbald, by the Manager of Covent Garden Theatre, for the Purpoſe of being adapted to Repreſentation—Satisfied, therefore, that the Work was in much more able Hands, ſhe totally relinquiſhed her Deſign.

On the firſt Night of the Repreſentation of LOVERS' VOWS, ſhe attended the Theatre, and confeſſes that ſhe was much ſurprized at the Extent of the Alterations and Omiſſions which had been made. She readily admits that theſe Alterations may have been neceſſary to accommodate the Play to the Taſte of an Engliſh Audience. Still, however, as ſhe is of opinion that the Piece has been diveſted of ſome of its principal Beauties, and that it does not reflect the Mind, the Principles, and the Genius of *Kotzebue*—

ſhe

ſhe feels herſelf irreſiſtibly prompted to preſent her favourite Author to the Public, in the Form he has choſen for himſelf, anxious that, as a Dramatic Writer, he ſhould be brought to a fair Trial at the Bar of Criticiſm. She wiſhes him to be exhibited in his own native Garb, not, as he emphatically expreſſes himſelf in his Preface, "in the borrowed Plumage of others," and that the Public may be enabled, at the ſame Time, to eſtimate the Merits of the Author, and appreciate the Value of the Alterations.

It will at once be candid and uſeful to enumerate the chief Points of Variation between the Play, as repreſented, and in its original Form.—

The moſt eſſential Deviation reſpects the important comic Character of the Count von der Mulde, which ſcarcely poſſeſſes a ſingle Feature of the Original. As it ſtands here, the Reader will obſerve, that it is a highly-wrought and exquiſitely finiſhed Portrait of a German Coxcomb. Whether this Character might have been reliſhed by an Engliſh Audience, the Tranſlator will not pretend to decide; her own Judgment, however, leads her to think that it would have had much more Effect in its original, than in its altered State. Diveſted of all its marked Features as a German Coxcomb, particularly of the French Phraſes ſo appropriate to that Character, yet not wholly transformed into an Engliſh *Petit Maitre*, we ſcarcely underſtand among what Deſcription of Perſons he is intended to be claſſed. The Baron, indeed, calls him a complete *Monkey*, but the ſmart Repartees put into his Mouth, ſeem wholly inconſiſtent with the Buffoonery beſpoken by that Appellation; he is, indeed, rather a witty Libertine than a Monkey. This very Appellation, however, is a Deviation from the Original, where he is called a Coxcomb; but perhaps this aroſe from a Miſtake of the Tranſlator's, between *Laffen* (a Coxcomb) and *Affen* (an Ape). Beſides this, from being one of the moſt prominent Perſonages in the Play, and deſigned as a forcible Contraſt to the plain and grave, but elevated Character of Frederick, he is now de-

2 graded

graded into a ſubordinate State, which leaves the Performance without a due Share of Comic Intereſt, and the happy Effect of the Contraſt is loſt. The laſt Scene between him and the Baron bears too much Reſemblance to that where Frederick diſcovers himſelf to the Baron as his Son, and conſequently has a Tendency to weaken the Effect of the latter Scene, which ought to have been preſerved as the moſt impreſſive in the whole Play.

The Amelia in LOVERS' VOWS, ſo far from being the artleſs, innocent Child of Nature, drawn by Kotzebue, appears a forward Country Hoyden, who deviates, in many Inſtances, from the eſtabliſhed Uſages of Society, and the Decorums of her Sex, in a Manner wholly unwarranted by the Original. The moſt amiable Traits in her Character are diſtorted and diſguiſed, by a Pertneſs which greatly detracts from the Eſteem which her benevolent Conduct would inſpire. Perhaps the latter may be better ſuited to Repreſentation before an Engliſh Audience, but in the Cloſet, the Amelia of Kotzebue

zebue will naturally excite the ſtronger Degree of Intereſt.

To the Alterations in the Character of the Butler, the Tranſlator can give her unqualified Approbation. He appears as decidedly a Gainer by the Garb in which Mrs. Inchbald has equipped him, as the Count and Amelia are Loſers. This Improvement, in ſome Degree, atones for the Loſs of humourous Effect in the Character of the Count; the doggrel Verſes are moſt happily introduced, and are an admirable Satire upon the namby-pamby Effuſions with which the Public is ſo profuſely preſented. The Tranſlator is ſenſible that thoſe here given from the original Play, will, in Compariſon, appear inſipid and defective in broad Humour.

Some intereſting Scenes and exquiſite Touches of Nature are omitted. This the Tranſlator has Reaſon to ſuſpect aroſe from the Imperfection of the Tranſlation put into Mrs. Inchbald's Hands.

In the Fifth Scene of the Firſt Act, the Benevolence of the Country Girl is not ſufficiently diſplayed, through the Omiſſion of the Paſſage

in

in which ſhe gives ſome Milk to the fainting Wilhelmina.

The Sixth and Seventh Scenes of the Firſt Act, and the Fifth Scene of the Fourth Act, are wholly ſuppreſſed.

The Fourth Scene in the Fourth Act opens very abruptly, in Conſequence of the Freedom with which the Pruning-knife has been wielded, by lopping off the firſt Half. The Reſt of the Omiſſions conſiſt of occaſional Curtailments in the Speeches and Dialogues.

The Tranſlation here given is from the genuine Leipſick Edition, publiſhed by the Author in 1791. Of the very great Reputation which this Play has acquired upon the Continent, ſome Idea may be formed from the Circumſtance, that, prior to the Appearance of that Publication, no leſs than twelve ſpurious and imperfect Editions had been publiſhed at Neuwied, Franckfort, Cologne, and Leipſick.

ANNE PLUMPTRE.

London, Oct. 15, 1798.

DRAMATIS PERSONÆ.

	Performed by
BARON VON WILDENHAIN, *a Colonel out of ſervice,* - - - -	Mr. MURRAY.
AMELIA, *his Daughter,* - - -	Mrs. H. JOHNSTON.
The PASTOR *of the Pariſh, in which lies the Baron's Eſtate, performed under the Name of* ANHALT*,	Mr. H. JOHNSTON.
COUNT VON DER MULDE, *performed under the Name of* COUNT CASSEL, - - - - - - - -	Mr. KNIGHT.
WILHELMINA BOETTCHER, *performed under the Name of* AGATHA FRIBOURG, - - - - - - -	Mrs. JOHNSON.
FREDERICK BOETTCHER, *a young Soldier, performed under the Name of* FREDERICK FRIBOURG,	Mr. POPE.
A Cottager, performed under the Name of HUBERT, - - - - -	Mr. POWEL.
COTTAGER'S WIFE, - - -	Mrs. DAVENPORT.
CHRISTIAN, *Butler in the* BARON'S *Family,* - - - - - - - -	Mr. MUNDEN.

LANDLORD *of the Public Houſe.*
A FARMER.
A LABOURER.
A YOUNG COUNTRY GIRL.
A JEW.
A HUNTSMAN.

SERVANTS *and* HUNTSMEN.

* This name, in the former Editions, is, by miſtake, called ARNAUD.

THE NATURAL SON.

ACT I.

SCENE I. *The Highway leading to a Town. The Road runs through a ſmall Village, the laſt Houſes of which are in Sight—A Public Houſe on the Right.*

Enter LANDLORD *from the Public Houſe, pulling* WILHELMINA *out by the arms.*

LANDLORD.

NO ſtaying here, woman, no ſtaying here!—It is the fair to day in the village, and as the country people paſs by with their wives and children, they'll be coming in, and I ſhall want every corner of my houſe.

Wilhel. Will you thruſt a poor ſick woman out of doors?

Land. I do not *thruſt* you out.

Wilhel. Your unkindneſs breaks my heart.

Land. It is no ſuch mighty hardſhip.

Wilhel. I have ſpent my laſt penny with you.

Land. You have—and becauſe it was your laſt, you can ſtay here no longer?

Wilhel. I can work.

Land. Why you can ſcarcely move your hands.

Wilhel. My ſtrength will return.

Land. Well, *then* you may return hither.

Wilhel. But what will become of me in the mean time?

Land. It is fine weather—you may be any where.

Wilhel. Who will clothe me ſhould this my only wretched garment be wet through with dew and rain?

Land. He who clothes the lilies of the field.

Wilhel. Who will give me a morſel of bread to appeaſe my hunger?

Land. He who feeds the fowls of the air.

Wilhel. Hard-hearted man! you know that I have faſted ever ſince yeſterday morning.

Land. The ſick can eat but little—eating is not good for them.

Wilhel. I will faithfully and honourably pay for every thing.

Land. By what means?—the times are hard.

Wilhel. My fate is alſo hard.

Land. I'll tell you what, woman—here lies the highway; the road is full of paſſengers—beg a ſmall matter of ſome pitiful heart.

Wilhel. Beg!—No—I will rather ſtarve!

Land. That's the great lady indeed!—but many an honeſt woman has begged for all that. Only try, cuſtom makes every thing eaſy.

(WILHELMINA *ſits down on a ſtone under a tree.)*

Land. And here comes ſomebody—I'll teach you how to begin.

SCENE II. *Enter a* LABOURER, *with his implements paſſing along the Road.*

Land. (to the Labourer) Good day!

Lab. Good day.

Land. Neighbour Nicholas, won't you pleaſe to beſtow a ſmall matter upon a poor woman. (*The Labourer paſſes off.)* That won't do. The poor devil muſt work himſelf for his daily pay. But here comes our fat Farmer, who every Sunday puts ſome money into the poor's-box, I'll lay a wager he gives you ſomething.

SCENE III. *Enter a jolly looking* FARMER, *who walks on very ſlowly.*

Land. Good day, Mr. Farmer! Fine weather!—Yonder ſits a poor ſick woman, who begs alms of you.

Farmer. Is ſhe not aſhamed of herſelf? She is ſtill young; ſhe can work.

Land. She has had the fever.

Farmer. Aye, one may work one's fingers to the bones; one may toil hard—but money is ſcarce enough now-a-days.

Land. Only beſtow a ſmall matter on her!—ſhe is hungry.

Farmer. (as he paſſes on) The harveſt has been very bad, and the diſtemper has carried off the beſt of my cattle. [*Exit.*

Land. There's a miſer for you, that does nothing but brood over his old dollars!—But talking of brooding, it comes into my head that my old hen hatches to day—I muſt make haſte and look after her.—*(Goes into the houſe.)*

SCENE IV. WILHELMINA *alone.—Her Clothes wretched, her Countenance bearing Marks of Sickneſs and Sorrow, yet ſtill retaining Traces of Beauty.*

Wilhel. O God! thou knoweſt that it was never thus with me while I had wherewithal to give!—Deareſt God! thou who haſt hitherto ſheltered me from deſpair, accept my thanks. Oh that I could but work again!—but this fever has ſo ſhaken me—did my Frederick know that his mother hungered!—Ah, lives he ſtill, or does a weight of earth now cover his remains?—Ah, no, no!—God forbid! I exiſt only to ſee him once more.—Thou author of my woes, I will not curſe thee; heaven ſuffer thee to proſper, if it can grant proſperity to the ſeducer of innocence!—Should chance conduct thee this way, ſhouldſt thou, amid theſe rags, beneath this ſorrow-ſtricken form, recognize thy formerly blooming Wilhelmina—what muſt be thy feelings?—Ah, I hunger; had I but a morſel of bread!—but patience; here on the highway I cannot long be ſuffered to want.

SCENE V. *Enter a young* COUNTRY GIRL, *carrying Eggs and Milk to Market—ſhe paſſes briſkly on, but ſeeing* WILHELMINA, *ſtops and ſpeaks.*

Country Girl. God preſerve you.

Wilhel. I thank you kindly!—Ah, deareſt child, have you not a morſel of bread to give to a poor woman?

Country Girl. (with looks of compaſſion) Bread! no, indeed, I have not any. Are you hungry then?

Wilhel. Alas, I am.

Country Girl. Ah, dearest God!—and I have no money, and I have eaten the very last morsel of my breakfast.---But I will hasten to the town, sell my milk and eggs, and when I return I will give you a *Dreyer.** But, now I think of it, all that time you will still be hungry.---Will you drink a little of my milk?

Wilhel. Oh, yes! and thank you kindly, tender-hearted girl.

Country Girl. Well, drink! drink! *(she holds the vessel up to her with much kindness)* Won't you have any more?—drink again if you like, you are heartily welcome.

Wilhel. Heaven reward you!—you have quite revived me.

Country Girl. I am heartily glad of it *(gives her a friendly nod)* good day, mother! God protect you!

[*Exit. singing.*

Wilhel. *(looking after her)* Such once was I—like her, brisk and joyous, and awake to pity.

SCENE VI. *Enter a* HUNTSMAN, *with his Gun and Dogs.*

Wilhel. Good sport to you, honest man!

Huntsman. *(as he passes on)* Damnation! must I be crossed on my way by an old woman at my first setting out!—I shall have no luck to day. The devil fetch you, you old witch. [*Exit.*

Wilhel. That fellow seeks to varnish over the hardness of his heart by his superstition.—But here comes another—a Jew—Ah, if I could beg—of him would I ask relief, for Christians do but *profess* humanity.

SCENE VII. *Enter a* JEW, *who is about to pass on, but seeing* WILHELMINA, *stops and examines her countenance.*

Wilhel. God bless you!

Jew. A thousand thanks, poor woman!—you seem very ill.

Wilhel. I have a fever.

Jew. *(feeling hastily in his pocket, whence he takes out a small purse, and gives her some money.)* Here, take this, 'tis all I can spare, I have not much myself. [*Exit.*

* About a halfpenny English. T.

Wilhel.

Wilhel. (much affected calls after him)—A thousand thanks! a thousand thanks!—Was I wrong?—Did my expectation deceive me?--the creed has no influence upon the heart.

SCENE VIII. FREDERICK *enters with his Knapsack at his Back, walks briskly on, humming a Tune: as he approaches, he observes the Sign of the Public-House, and stops.*

Fred. Humph!--to drink!---it is very hot to-day. --But let me first examine my purse.—*(takes out some pieces of money, which he contemplates as he holds them in his hand)* Yes, to be sure there will be enough to pay for a breakfast and a dinner, and by evening, please God, I hope to be at home. Come, then, I am very thirsty--- Holla! Landlord! *(he sees Wilhelmina)* But what have we here? a poor sick woman, pining, consuming away--- she does not beg, but her situation asks assistance, and should we always wait to give till we are entreated?— fye, fye!—We must forego the drinking, else shall we have nothing left for dinner; be it so!—To perform a good action satisfies both hunger and thirst —There! (*goes to her intending to give her the money, which he was holding between his fingers to pay for his liquor.*)

Wilhel. (*looks at him stedfastly, then gives a loud shriek*) —Frederick!!!

Fred. (*starts, gazes at her earnestly, throws away his money, knapsack, hat, stick, whatever encumbers him, and falls into her arms*) Mother!!! (*both remain speechless some time—Frederick first recovers himself and proceeds*)--- Mother! Good heavens! to find you in this state!--- Mother!—what is the matter!—speak!

Wilhel. (*trembling*) I cannot—speak—dear son!--- dear Frederick!—the joy!--the transport!

Fred. Recover yourself, dear, dear mother! (*he rests her head upon his breast*) Recover yourself! how you tremble!—you are fainting.

Wilhel. I am so weak---my head is so giddy---the whole of yesterday—I had nothing to eat.

Fred. *(starting up, wildly, and covering his face with both hands)* Ah, my God! *(he runs to his knapsack, tears*

it

it open, and takes out a piece of bread) here is bread! *(collects together the money which he had thrown away, and adds what remained in his pocket)* here is my little ſtore of money, and my coat, my cloak, my arms, I'll ſell them all. Ah, mother, mother.—Holla, Landlord! *(knocks haſtily at the public-houſe).*

Landlord. (looking out at the window) What's the matter?

Fred. A bottle of wine here!—quick!—diſpatch!

Land. A bottle of wine!

Fred. Yes, yes!

Land. And for whom?

Fred. For me!—the devil!—make haſte!

Land. Well, well!—but, Mr. Soldier, can you pay for it?

Fred. Here is money!—but make haſte, or I'll break every window in your houſe.

Land. Patience! patience! *(he ſhuts the window).*

Fred. (to his mother) Faſted the whole day!—faſted!—and I had wherewithal to eat!—I had a good ſupper ſerved up to me yeſterday evening at the Inn, while my mother hungered!—Oh, God! how is all my promiſed joy embittered!

Wilhel. Be comforted, dear Frederick!—I ſee thee again—I am now well—I have been very ill—I ſcarcely hoped ever to ſee thee more.

Fred. Ill! and I was not with you!—Well, never will I leave you more.—See, I am become tall, and ſtrong, I will work for your ſupport.

Enter LANDLORD *with a bottle and glaſs.*

Land. There is wine—of precious growth; a glorious bottle; 'tis only Franconian wine to be ſure, but it is ſour enough to paſs for good old Rheniſh.

Fred. Bring it hither! What does the traſh coſt?

Land. Traſh! call one of the moſt precious gifts of Heaven traſh! Good friend my wine is no traſh; I have beſides another delicious French wine in my cellar, aye, you ought to taſte that, ſo rich, ſo luſcious, when you have emptied the glaſs it looks dyed all over ſuch a fine red. *(Frederick impatiently attempts to ſnatch the bottle from*

from him) Come, come, I muſt have the money firſt! this bottle coſts half a guilder*.

Fred. (Gives him all his money) There! there! *(pours out ſome for his mother, who drinks, and eats a piece of bread with it.)*

Land. (Counting over the money) It is one dreyer ſhort, but however one ought to be compaſſionate—To revive a poor ſick woman, one may overlook ſuch a thing; but take care of the bottle, and do not break the glaſs, there's a fine German verſe engrav'd upon it. [*Exit.*

Wilhel. I thank thee kindly, deareſt Frederick! wine is reviving, and wine, *from the hands of a ſon*, gives new life.

Fred. Don't exhauſt yourſelf by talking, mother; recover yourſelf!

Wilhel. Tell me then how it has fared with you for theſe laſt five years?

Fred. Good and ill jumbled together; one day 'twas all plenty, the next nothing at all.

Wilhel. 'Tis a long time ſince you have written to me.

Fred. Ah deareſt mother 'tis a hard matter for a poor ſoldier to afford the money for poſtage, only think of the diſtance—it takes half a year's pay, and you know one muſt live. And then I always thought within myſelf, my mother is ſtrong and healthy, and I am ſtrong and healthy, I may as well wait a few weeks longer; and ſo I delayed it from one week to another,—but I hope you'll forgive me, deareſt mother.

Wilhel. We eaſily forgive neglect when the anxiety it occaſions is no longer felt. Have you then obtained your diſcharge?

Fred. No. I have only procured leave of abſence for a few months for a particular reaſon; but you want me, I will continue with you.

Wilhel. There is no occaſion, dear Frederick,—your viſit will reſtore my health and renew my vigour, then ſhall I be able again to work, and you may return to your regiment; I would not be a hindrance to your fortune. But it ſeems you have obtained leave of abſence for a *particular reaſon?* Did you not ſay ſo?—may I know this reaſon?

* About thirteen pence Engliſh. T.

Fred.

Fred. Oh yes, dear mother!—liſten and I will relate it.—When I left you five years ago, you equipped me excellently with clothes, and linen, and money,—but one trifle you forgot,—the certificate of my birth. I was at that time a giddy, thoughtleſs lad of fifteen, and this never occurred to me, but it has ſince occaſioned me much vexation. Many times have I been heartily weary of a ſoldier's buſtling life, and was deſirous of obtaining my diſcharge, that I might apply myſelf to learning ſome reputable trade, but whenever I mentioned this ſubject to any tradeſman, ſaying, "Good Sir, I wiſh to bind myſelf to you to learn your trade," the firſt queſtion always was, "where's the certificate of your birth?"—That ſettled the point at once. I was vexed and continued a ſoldier, for in that profeſſion they only aſk, whether all is right about the heart; the certificate of birth is of no more account than the diploma of nobility. But ſtill this brought me into many unpleaſant ſcrapes. My comrades found this out, and if any of them wiſhed to teaze me, or were intoxicated, they would ſneer at me, and make ill-natured ſpeeches, and endeavour to irritate me. Twice I was even compelled to fight, and was put under arreſt. My captain frequently admoniſhed me.—and at laſt about five weeks ago, when another of theſe quarrels happened, he called me to him in his own room—(Oh, mother, my captain is a fine charming man) —"Boettcher," ſaid he, "I am ſorry to learn, that you are continually getting into quarrels and incurring puniſhment, for in other reſpects I am extremely ſatisfied with your ſervice, and have a good opinion of you. The ſerjeant has informed me of the cauſe. I'll tell you what—write home, and deſire that your certificate may be ſent, or if you are inclined to go and fetch it yourſelf, I will give you leave of abſence for a few months,—the time of exerciſing is over."—Oh, mother, your form hovered before my eyes, as he ſpoke ſo kindly. I kiſſed his hand and ſtammered out my thanks. He preſented me with a dollar,—"Go, my lad," ſaid he, "may your journey be proſperous, and remember to return at the proper time."—Now, mother, you ſee I am here, and this is the whole of the ſtory.

Wilhel. (who had liſtened to his narrative with embarraſsment.) And you are come hither, dear Frederick, to fetch the certificate of your birth?

Wilhel.

Fred. Yes.

Wilhel. Oh heavens!

Fred. What is the matter? *(Wilhelmina burſts into tears)* for God's ſake what is the matter?

Wilhel. Alas, you can have no ſuch certificate!

Fred. How?

Wilhel. You are—a—NATURAL SON——

Fred. So, ſo!—and who then is my father?

Wilhel. Ah! the wildneſs of your looks tortures me!

Fred. *(recovering himſelf and ſpeaking mildly and affectionately)* Be not alarmed, deareſt mother!—ſtill I am your ſon—tell me only who is my father?

Wilhel. When you left me five years ago, you were too young to be entruſted with ſuch a ſecret. Now your maturer years demand my confidence. You are grown to man's eſtate, and are moreover worthy of the name of man. My fair maternal hopes have not deceived me. Ah, I have heard full often, how conſolatory, how reviving it is to the ſpirits of the afflicted to meet with one to whom their wrongs may be imparted. The tears which thoſe ſufferings draw from the eyes of another, aſſuage the anguiſh of the ſufferer. Thanks, thanks be to God the hour is arrived, in which I can enjoy this conſolation: my ſon is my confident, be he alſo my judge, for a ſtrict judge I muſt deprecate, but my ſon will not be ſevere on me.——

Fred. Speak, deareſt mother! lay open your whole heart!

Wilhel. Ah my ſon, I will tell you all; and yet ſhame almoſt chains my tongue: do not then look at me.

Fred. Know I not well the heart of my mother! accurſed be the thought that would condemn her for a *weakneſs*——of a *crime* ſhe is incapable.

Wilhel. Yon village, the ſpire of whoſe church you ſee at a diſtance, is the place of my birth: In that church was I baptized, and there alſo was I inſtructed in the firſt rudiments of our faith. My parents were pious and good cottagers; poor, but honeſt. When I was fourteen years old, I chanced one day to be ſeen by the lady of the caſtle: I pleaſed her, ſhe took me to her manſion, and delighted in forming my ruſtic mind. She put good books into my hands; I was inſtructed in French and muſic; my ideas and capacity for learning developed themſelves, but ſo alſo did my vanity: Yes, under the appearance of reserve I became a vain silly girl. I had just attained my seventeenth year, when the son of my benefactress, who was in the Saxon service, obtained leave of absence, and came to visit us; it was the first time of my seeing him; he was a handsome and engaging youth;—he talked to me of love, of marriage;—he was the first man who had paid homage to my charms: Ah, Frederick, do not look at me, I cannot go on.

Fred. (casts down his eyes, and presses her hand to his heart—both pause.)

Wilhel. I, too credulous creature, was beguiled of my innocence! he feigned the most ardent love—promised me marriage after the death of his aged mother---swore eternal faith and constancy.—Alas! and I forgot my pious parents, the precepts of our worthy pastor, the kindness of my foster-mother—Ah Frederick, Frederick, often as I cast my eyes towards the tower of yonder church, so often does the figure of our good old pastor with his silver hairs seem to stand before my eyes, as he appeared when for the first time I went to confession. How did my young heart then flutter—how full was I of virtue and elevated devotion!—Oh at that time, certain of triumph, I had courage frankly to acknowledge every failing.—How, good Heavens! how could it be possible, that a wild, unthinking youth, should, by a few idle words and glances, efface that deep, deep impression: yet so it was—I became pregnant.—We were both awakened from our sweet intoxication, and shuddered at the fearful prospect of the future. I had put every thing to the hazard—he only had to fear the anger of his mother, a good, but inexorably strict woman. How tenderly did he conjure me, how affectingly did he entreat of me, not to betray him!—How impressively, how ardently did he promise hereafter to make me amends for all---and so dearly did I love him, that I gave him my word, to conceal the name of my seducer,—to bury his image in my heart, and patiently to endure, for his sake, whatever sorrow might be in store for me.---Alas 'tis much indeed that I have suffered!---He departed, satisfied---meanwhile the time of my delivery approached---I could no longer conceal my situation---Ah I was severely dealt with for persisting in my refusal to name the father of my child.---I was driven indignantly from the house, and when I came to the door

of

of my afflicted parents, there too was I denied admittance. My father upbraided me bitterly, and even was about to curſe me, when my mother tore him haſtily away. She ſoon returned—threw me a crooked dollar, which ſhe wore about her neck, and wept; ſince that time I never have ſeen them. But the dollar I have ſtill *(ſhe draws it out from her boſom.)* I have ſuffered hunger rather than part with this! *(ſhe gazes on it ſome time, kiſſes it, and reſtores it to its place.)* Without a houſe in which to hide my head, without money, without friends, I wandered a whole night in the open fields. Once I had arrived at the river-ſide, there where ſtands the mill, and ſorely was I tempted to throw myſelf in under the mill-wheel, thus at once to end my miſery. But immediately the image of the worthy Paſtor preſented itſelf before me with his gentle, venerable mien.—I ſtarted back, and looked around to ſee whether he were not behind me.—The thought of him, and of his precepts, awakened my confidence—morning came on, I reſolved to go to his houſe. He received me affectionately, uttered not a ſingle reproach—"What is done," he ſaid, "is done! Heaven pardons the penitent—reform then, my daughter, and all may yet be well. Here in this village, however, thou muſt not remain; that will be to thee a continued mortification, and a ſcandal to my pariſhioners——but,"—and here he put a piece of gold into my hand, together with a letter which he had written in my behalf,—"go to the town, my daughter, ſeek out an old and reſpectable widow to whom this letter is directed, with her thou wilt be ſafe, and ſhe will beſides give thee inſtruction in what manner to obtain an honeſt livelihood."—With theſe words he laid his hand upon my forehead, and giving me his bleſſing, promiſed alſo to endeavour to ſoften my father.—Ah I ſeemed now to receive new life!—On my way to the town I reconciled myſelf with my Creator, and ſolemnly vowed never again to deviate from the path of virtue—that vow I have ſtrictly kept, ſo far may you ſtill reſpect me, my Frederick. *(Frederick preſſes her ſilently in his arms, after a pauſe ſhe proceeds)* Your birth was to me the cauſe of much ſorrow, and much joy—Twice did I write to your father, but God only knows whether he received the letters, no anſwer have I ever obtained.

 Fred.

Fred. (*Haſtily*) No anſwer!

Wilhel. Be calm! my ſon, be calm!---It was in time of war, his regiment was then in ſervice,---all was buſtle and confuſion throughout the whole country,---the troops of three different powers purſued each other alternately; how eaſily then might letters be loſt; No, he certainly never received mine, for he was no villain. Since then indeed I have never troubled him; it might be pride, or call it what you pleaſe, but I thought that if he had not forgotten me, he would certainly ſeek information concerning me,---learn from our paſtor whither I was retired, and come to ſee me, but alas, he came not, and ſome years after I even heard (*ſhe ſighs deeply*)---that he was married. Thus was I compelled to bid farewel to my laſt ray of hope;---in ſolitude and obſcurity I inhabited an indigent cottage, where I gained a livelihood by the work of my hands, and by inſtructing the neighbouring children in what I had learnt at the caſtle. You, my deareſt Frederick, were my only joy; and on your education I beſtowed all that I could ſpare from the neceſſaries of food and clothing. My diligence was not ill repaid; you were a good boy, only your wildneſs, your youthful fire, your love for a ſoldier's life, and deſire to ramble about the world, occaſioned me many a heartache: at laſt I thought it muſt be as God pleaſes! Is it the boy's deſtination? I will not hinder him, though my heart ſhould break at the ſeparation. Five years ago therefore, I ſuffered you to depart, giving you at that time, all that I could poſſibly ſpare, perhaps more than I ought to have ſpared, but I was then in health, and when that is the caſe, one is too apt to think that ſickneſs never can come. Indeed had I continued well, I had ſtill earnt much more than I wanted for myſelf, had been a rich woman for one in my ſituation, and ſtill, dear Frederick, had ſent you every year a Chriſtmas preſent. But I was attacked by a lingering illneſs---there ended my earnings---my little ſtore ſcarcely ſufficed for phyſician, nurſe, and medicines, and I was obliged a few days ago, to turn my back upon my poor little cottage, as I had no longer wherewithal to pay the rent. My only reſource was to totter along the road with this ſtick, this bag, and theſe rags, and ſolicit a morſel of bread from the charity of thoſe who happened to paſs by.

Fred. Ah, if your Frederick had ſuſpected this, how bitter would have been every morſel he eat, every drop that he drank. Well, God be thanked! I am here again, you are alive, and I will remain with you; I will not on any account leave you; and I will write thus to my Captain. Let him take it as he will, let him revile it as deſertion, I will not ſtir from my mother. Alas! however I have not learnt any art, any trade, but I have a pair of nervous arms, I can guide the plough, I can handle the flail; I will hire myſelf as a day-labourer, and at night copy writings for ſome lawyer; for thanks to you, my good mother, I write a fair and legible hand. Oh, all will go well! God will help us, for he ſupports thoſe who honour their parents.

Wilhel. (claſps him in her arms much affected) What princeſs could offer me an equivalent for ſuch a ſon?

Fred. One thing you have ſtill forgotten, mother— What is my father's name?

Wilhel. Baron Wildenhain.

Fred. And he lives on this eſtate?

Wilhel. Here once lived his mother, but ſhe is dead. He himſelf married a noble heireſs in Franconia, and as I am aſſured, has, to pleaſe her, for ever forſaken his native country. A Steward, in the mean time, lives in the houſe, who manages the eſtate at his pleaſure.

Fred. I will haſten to the Baron my father—I will boldly face him— I will bear you upon my back to him. How great is the diſtance of Franconia; from twenty to thirty miles*? only ſo far has he removed himſelf, and has he eſcaped from his conſcience at ſo ſhort a diſtance? Truly, a lazy creeping kind of a conſcience, twenty years has it been crawling after him, and not yet overtaken him!---Oh, ſhame! ſhame!---Wherefore muſt I know my father, when my father is not an honeſt man? My heart was ſatisfied with a mother, a mother who has taught me to love, and why ſhould I know a father who will teach me to hate?---No, I will not ſeek him!---Let him remain where he is, and feaſt and pamper himſelf till his laſt hour, and then he may ſee how he has prepared himſelf to meet his God. Is it not true, mother, that we need him not? We will —— but what is the matter! your countenance is changed!---Mother, what is the matter?

* A German mile is equal to about five Engliſh. T.

Wilhel.

Wilhel. *(very weak and almoſt fainting)* Nothing nothing!—my joy!—too much talking!—I wiſh to be quiet awhile.

Fred. My God! I never till now perceived that we were in the high way! *(he knocks at the door of the public-houſe)* Halloo! Landlord!

Land. *(at the window)* Well, what is the matter now?

Fred. Here, I want a bed in an inſtant for this poor woman.

Land. A bed for this poor woman! *(ſneeringly)* Ha, ha, ha!—Laſt night ſhe lay in the ſtall with my cattle, and has bewitched them all! *(ſhuts the window)*.

Fred. *(taking up a ſtone in a rage)* Curſed ſcoundrel! *(he looks at his mother and drops the ſtone again)* Ah, my poor mother! *(he knocks in deſpairing anguiſh at a cottage door which ſtands further in the back groud)* Halloo! halloo!

SCENE IX. *Enter a* COTTAGER *from the Houſe.*

Cottager. God preſerve you!—What do you want?

Fred. Good friend, look at this poor woman, ſhe is fainting here in the open air. She is my mother. Do pray let her have a corner in your houſe, where ſhe may reſt for half an hour. I beg it for God's ſake, and heaven will reward you!

Cottager. Hold your tongue, I entreat!—I underſtand you perfectly well *(ſpeaking to ſomebody in the houſe)* Bet, make up the bed there, quickly; you can lay the boy upon the bench in the mean time: *(to Frederick)* Don't tell me a long ſtory again about God rewarding, and heaven paying; if God is to pay all ſuch trifles, he'll have enough to do indeed. Come, quick, ſupport her, let us lead her in gently. A bed, as good as I can give her, ſhe ſhall have; but indeed ſhe will not find much in my houſe beſides. *(They lead her into the cottage)*.

END OF THE FIRST ACT.

ACT II.

SCENE I. *A Room in the Cottage.*

WILHELMINA, FREDERICK, *the* COTTAGER *and his* WIFE.

WILHELMINA *ſits on a wooden Stool, with her Head ſupported on her Son's Breaſt.*

FREDERICK *(ſpeaking to the Cottager and his Wife, as they are buſied about the Cottage.)*

FREDERICK.

DEAR good people, have you nothing then? Nothing ſtrengthening? nothing reviving?

Wife. Run, huſband, to our neighbour at the public houſe, and fetch a bottle of wine.

Fred. Ah, that will not do!—his wine is as bad as his heart. She has already tried that, and I fear it has proved poiſon to her.

Cottager. Go and ſee, wife, whether the black hen has not laid an egg. A new laid egg boiled ſoft——

Wife. Or a few ripe currants——

Cottager. Or, the beſt thing that I have——a piece of bacon.

Wife. Or, there's about half a pint of brandy ſtanding in the dairy.

Fred. (much affected.) God bleſs you and reward you for your kind-heartedneſs!—Do you hear mother *(Wilhelmina nods her head)*—Do you like any of theſe things? *(Wilhelmina makes a motion with her hand declining them)* She does not fancy them—is there no phyſician in the neighbourhood?

Cottager. There's a horſe doctor lives in the village—but I never in my life ſaw any other.

Fred.

Fred. Oh God what ſhall I do!—ſhe will die in my arms—merciful God, take pity on me!—Kind people pray for us—pray i entreat you! I cannot pray myſelf.

Wilhel. (with a broken voice.) Be comforted dear Frederick—I am well—I am only faint, very faint—a glaſs of good wine——

Fred. Yes mother!—immediately mother—directly! But, oh God where ſhall I procure it!—no money—none, not a doit.

Wife. Look you here, huſband—did you carry the money for the rent yeſterday to the ſteward?

Cottager. Yes, indeed, the more's the pity. What can be done!—It is true, as I am an honeſt man, that I have not a ſingle doit in the houſe.

Fred. I will—I will beg—and if I cannot ſucceed by begging, I will rob!—Good people, take care of my poor mother—do what you are able!---give her what help you can!---I will ſoon return. *(Ruſhes out of the houſe.)*

SCENE II. WILHELMINA, *the* COTTAGER, *and his* WIFE.

Cottager. Should he but ſtep to our paſtor, he'll give ſomething for certain.

Wilhel. Does the worthy old paſtor then ſtill live?

Wife. Alas no!---The good old gentleman!---it has pleaſed God to take him—he died two years ago, worn out and weary of life.

Cottager. He went out like a lamp.

Wife. (wiping her eyes) We have reaſon enough to weep for him.

Cottager. (with tears alſo) He was our father.

Wilhel. (extremely affected) Our father!

Wife. We ſhall never have ſuch another.

Cottager. Well, well! let every man have his due—we muſt not cry down any body. Our preſent paſtor is alſo a worthy good man.

Wife. Yes, indeed, huſband—but very young.

Cottager. 'Tis true, one can't look up to him with quite ſo much reſpect—our hearts don't take to him ſo readily—but our old paſtor himſelf, you know, was once young.

Wife.

Wife. (to Wilhelmina) This gentleman was tutor in the family, and my lord the Baron was ſo well ſatisfied with him, that he made him our paſtor.

Cottager. And well he might be ſatisfied; for to be ſure our young lady, God bleſs her, is a charming, affable creature.

Wife. Not at all proud. When ſhe comes to church, ſhe nods her head round to all the countrywomen, firſt to one and then to another.

Cottager. And when ſhe comes into the pew, ſhe holds her fan before her face, and prays with ſuch devotion!

Wife. And during the ſermon, ſhe never once turns away her eyes from the paſtor.

Wilhel. (with emotion) And who is this young lady?

Cottager. The daughter of my lord the Baron.

Wilhel. Is ſhe here, then?

Wife. Here!—yes, to be ſure!—did not you know that?—Next Friday it will be five weeks ſince his lordſhip made his entry into the Caſtle, bag and baggage.

Wilhel. Baron Wildenhain?

Wife. Yes, my lord himſelf.

Wilhel. And his lady?

Cottager. Oh, no; her ladyſhip is dead. They lived ſome hundred miles off, in Franconia; and while her ladyſhip was alive, my lord never came amongſt us. That has frequently been a great loſs to us. *(Speaking in a ſort of whiſper.)* She was a proud kind of lady, with a heap of fancies. Well, well, we ſhould not ſpeak ill of the dead. The Baron is ſtill a very good kind of gentleman;—ſcarcely had my lady cloſed her eyes, when he reſolved immediately to leave the place, and returned to Wildenhain. And well he might, for this is his native place;—here he grew up to manhood; many a time has he joined in our country ſports, and has often danced with my wife on a Sunday evening under the lime-trees.——Don't you remember it, Bet?

Wife. O yes, to be ſure, I may well remember it. The young gentleman uſed to wear a red coat, and fine buckles ſet with ſparkling ſtones.

Cottager. Afterwards, indeed, when he became an officer, he turned out rather wild; but young folks muſt ſow their wild oats; the ſoil was naturally good, but the richeſt earth, you know, will ſometimes bear weeds.

Wife. But do you remember, huſband, what a piece of work he made with Boettcher's Minny?—That was not right.

Cottager. Huſh, wife! we muſt not bring up ſuch old ſtories. Beſides, we don't know that he was the father of her child; ſhe never ſaid ſo.

Wife. Well, for all that, I'd lay my Sunday gown and laced cap that he was the man, and nobody elſe.— No, no, huſband, you muſt not defend that—that was wicked. Who knows whether the poor creature has not died of hunger and grief—and her poor father, old Boettcher, he might have lived longer, if he had not been ſo heart-broken about it. *(Wilhelmina faints.)*

Cottager. (firſt perceiving her) Bet! Bet!—Help! Zounds, help!

Wife. Ah! my God!—poor woman!

Cottager. Quick, quick, carry her into the chamber; lay her on the bed—and then we'll go and fetch the paſtor, for ſhe ſcarcely can live till morning.

(They carry her in.)

SCENE III. *A Room in the* BARON'*s Caſtle.*

The Breakfaſt-table is ſet out, a lighted Candle and a Roll of wax Taper on the Table.

The BARON *enters in his night gown.*

Baron. Sleeps the Count ſtill?

Servant. No, my lord; his hair is already dreſſed.

Baron. I ſuſpected ſo; the whole houſe is ſcented with *poudre à la Marechalle.* Call my daughter hither. *(The ſervant goes out, the Baron fills his pipe and lights it.)*— It ſeems to me that the old privy-counſellor has ſaddled me with a complete coxcomb; whatever he ſays and does, is as ſilly and conceited as his countenance.—No, I will not be precipitate—my Amelia is too dear to me for that;—I muſt firſt know the young gentleman a little better, and not for the ſake of an ancient friendſhip make my daughter unhappy. The poor girl innocently ſays yes, and ſhe will do as her father pleaſes, and he under-ſtands

ſtands theſe things better than herſelf. Pity, pity, indeed, that the girl was not a boy!---Pity that the name of Wildenhain muſt be extinct, even as the flame which I now blow out.---*(He blows out the candle with which he had lighted his pipe.)*---All my fine eſtates, my glorious proſpects, my honeſt, well-conditioned tenants---all, all muſt paſs into foreign hands!---'tis to be regretted---much to be regretted!

SCENE IV. *Enter* AMELIA *in a looſe morning dreſs.*

Amelia. (kiſſing the Baron's hand) Good morrow, dear father.

Baron. Good morrow, my daughter. You have ſlept well, I hope?

Amelia. Oh! yes.

Baron. You have, indeed, ſlept well? Not been at all diſturbed?

Amelia. No—only the gnats made rather a humming in my ears.

Baron. The gnats! Well, that does not much ſignify. We muſt only ſmoke a bough of juniper in the room. 'Tis eaſier to drive away gnats than maggots.

Amelia. If you want to drive them away, 'tis only to boil ſome peas with a little quickſilver, and that will kill them.

Baron. (laughing) Well, well, it will be happy for you, Amelia, if you never know any other maggots than what a plate of peas will kill.

Amelia. Oh, you mean maggots in the head! No, no, I have none of them.

Baron. So much the better. What, indeed, ſhould a young, lively girl of ſixteen like you, have to do with maggots in her head. You have a father who loves you tenderly, and a ſuitor who begs permiſſion to love you. How do you like the Count von der Mulde?

Amelia. Very well.

Baron. Do you not bluſh when I name him?

Amelia. (feeling her cheeks) No.

Baron. No!—Humph!---And you have not dreamt of him?

Amelia. No.

Baron. You did not dream at all, perhaps?

Amelia. (*conſidering*) Oh! yes, I dreamt of our paſtor.

Baron. Aha! as he ſtood before you, and aſked you for the ring?

Amelia. Oh, no! not ſo.—I dreamt that we were ſtill in Franconia, and he was ſtill my tutor, and was about to depart, and that I wept bitterly.

Baron. And that your father laughed, and your mother ſcolded?—Is it not true?—Yes, yes, it was a fooliſh ſcene.—It is ſtill perfectly in my remembrance.

Amelia. And when I waked, my eyes were really wet.

Baron. Hear me, Amelia! When you dream again of the paſtor, let it be that he ſtood at the altar, and you and the Count ſtood before him, and exchanged rings*. What think you of that?

Amelia. I will moſt certainly, dear father, if you command it.

Baron. The devil!---No, I do not *command* it!---But I wiſh to know whether you love him? You know you ſaw him at the ball, when we ſpent a few days in town laſt winter.

Amelia. Should I then love every body whom I ſee at a ball?

Baron. Amelia! Amelia! Do not be ſtupid!---I mean, that at that time the Count von der Mulde ſimpered and ogled with you—danced an elegant minuet or two together—he poured *eau de mille fleurs* upon your pocket-handkerchief, and God knows what he was talking about all the time.

Amelia. God knows, indeed!—I'm ſure I remember nothing about it.

Baron. Nothing?

Amelia. If it would be a ſatisfaction to you, I will endeavour to recollect as much as I can.

Baron. No, no, there is no occaſion. What one is forced to *try* to recollect, can only be brought forth from a corner of the memory, not from the receſſes of the heart. You do not then love him?

Amelia. I believe not.

* In Germany, it is the practice, in the marriage ceremony, for the bride and bridegroom to exchange rings.——T.

Baron.

Baron. (aside.) I believe not too.---Yet I wiſh to make you underſtand the connection between his viſit and my queſtions. His father is a privy-counſellor—a man of wealth and rank---of wealth and rank! doſt thou hear?

Amelia. Yes, dear father—if you command it. But our paſtor always told me that I ſhould not regard ſuch things; that wealth and rank are mere gifts of chance.

Baron. Well, well, he is right enough in that. But if it ſo happen that wealth and rank go hand in hand with merit, then they are an advantage. You underſtand me?

Amelia. Perfectly. *(With ſimplicity, and without any apparent deſign.)* And is that the caſe with the Count von der Mulde?

Baron. (embarraſſed.) Humph!---His father has rendered the State important ſervices;—he is my old friend—he forwarded my ſuit with your mother, and I have great obligations to him; and becauſe he ſo earneſtly wiſhes for a marriage between you and his ſon---and becauſe he ſuppoſes that in time you will love the young man ſo ardently——

Amelia. Does he ſuppoſe that?

Baron. Yes. But it appears to me that you are not of the ſame opinion?

Amelia. Not entirely. Still, if you command, dear father——

Baron. The devil!—I tell you that one muſt not *command* in ſuch things;----a marriage without love is like ſlavery in the galleys;—none but congenial minds ſhould be united—I would not pair a nightingale with a finch. If you like each other, be it ſo---if not, here let the matter reſt. *(More calmly.)* Attend, my Amelia!—the whole of the affair is this—can you, or can you not, love this man? If you cannot, then we muſt ſend him back with a refuſal.

Amelia. Dear father, it appears to me that I never ſhall love him. I have read ſo much in romances about love, how ſtrange and wonderful are its effects——

Baron. Hey! what! Don't prattle to me of your romances! they are the devil, indeed!—they tell you a parcel of nonſenſe, that never can ſtand the teſt of experience. But ſtop!—I will put a few queſtions to you—anſwer them with ſincerity, Amelia—with ſtrict ſincerity.

Amelia.

Amelia. I have never anſwered you otherwiſe.

Baron. Are you pleaſed when you hear people talk of the Count?

Amelia. Good or ill?

Baron. Good, good?

Amelia. Oh, yes. I am always pleaſed when I hear good of any man.

Baron. But are you not elated when you hear him mentioned? *(She ſhakes her head.)* Are you not embarraſſed? *(She ſhakes her head.)* Do you not wiſh ſometimes that he ſhould be made the ſubject of converſation, yet have not courage to begin talking of him yourſelf? *(She ſhakes her head.)* Would you not defend him, if you ſhould hear him calumniated?

Amelia. Oh, certainly, if I could. Our paſtor——

Baron. Pſhaw! Pſhaw! we won't talk about our paſtor at preſent.—How do you feel when you ſee the Count?

Amelia. Very well.

Baron. Don't you feel any palpitation as he approaches you?

Amelia. No. *(Haſtily recollecting herſelf.)* Yes, I did once.

Baron. Aha!—now it's coming out.

Amelia. It was at the ball, when he trod on my foot.

Baron. Don't be fooliſh, Amelia!—Don't you caſt down your eyes when he addreſſes you?

Amelia. I never caſt my eyes down before any body.

Baron. Do you not play with your apron or handkerchief, when he is talking to you?

Amelia. No.

Baron. Does not your face glow when he makes you a fine ſpeech, referring perhaps to love or marriage?

Amelia. Did he ever ſay any thing of that kind to me? 'Tis more than I recollect.

Baron. Humph! humph!——*(After a pauſe.)* Have you not ſometimes yawned while he was talking to you?

Amelia. No, dear father—that is not polite.

Baron. But were you ever diſpoſed to yawn?

Amelia. Oh yes, dear father.

Baron. So!—then there is little hope.—Do you think him handſome?

Amelia. I don't know.

Baron.

Baron. Do not you know what beauty is?—or do you not know whether you think *him* handſome?

Amelia. I never particularly examined him.

Baron. Bad again.—How did you feel when he came yeſterday evening?

Amelia. I was vexed;—for at the very time the ſervant ſo unſeaſonably called me, I was walking with our paſtor on the little romantic hill.

Baron. Unſeaſonably!—Humph!——Well, only one more queſtion.—Have you not undeſignedly dreſſed your hair this morning with unuſual care, and ſelected a particularly becoming deſhabille?

Amelia. *(ſurveying herſelf)* This is not dirty yet, dear father; I only wore it yeſterday and the day before.

Baron. *(aſide)* Here is, indeed, little proſpect of ſucceſs! Well, my dear child, the Count, then, is indifferent to you?

Amelia. Why, yes—unleſs you command—

Baron. *(warmly)* Liſten to me, Amelia!—If you repeat again your damned *command*, I may be tempted perhaps to *command* indeed. *(More mildly.)* To ſee you happy, my child, is my earneſt wiſh, and *commands* cannot produce happineſs. Marriage is a very inharmonious duet, if the tones are ill aſſorted; therefore the great Compoſer has planted in our hearts the pure harmony of love. I'll tell you what, Amelia, I will ſend the paſtor to you.

Amelia. *(joyfully)* The paſtor!

Baron. He ſhall inſtruct you in the duties of the marriage ſtate; for that office a clergyman is better qualified than a father.—Then examine yourſelf; and if you believe that the Count is the man towards whom your heart can fulfil theſe duties, in God's name marry him.—Till then I ſay no more. *(calls)* Henry! *(a ſervant enters)* Go to the paſtor, and deſire him, if he be diſengaged, to come hither for a quarter of an hour. *(The ſervant is going.)*

Amelia. And tell him, I wiſh him a good morning.

Baron. *(looking at his watch)* My young gentleman takes a deviliſh time for dreſſing, methinks. Come, Amelia, pour out the tea.

(Amelia ſits down at the tea-table.)

Baron. What ſort of weather have we?—Have you put your head out of the window this morning Amelia?

Amelia.

Amelia. Oh, I was in the garden by five o'clock; it is indeed a moſt charming morning.

Baron. One may then take an hour's ſhooting; I know not what elſe to do with my gentleman—he fatigues me terribly. Ha! here he comes!

SCENE V. *Enter* COUNT *von der* MULDE.

Count. Ah, *bon jour mon colonel!*—Dear young lady, I kiſs your hand. *(Amelia curtſies.)*

Baron. Good morrow! good morrow! Why, count, it is almoſt noon. In the country one is uſed to riſe earlier.

Count. **Pardonnez, mon colonel!*—I have been up ever ſince ſix o'clock; but my *homme de chambre* has been guilty of a *betiſe*, which has quite driven me to deſpair—a loſs which *pour le moment* cannot be repaired.

Baron. Aye! aye! I am ſorry indeed for that. *(Amelia offers him tea.)*

Count. (*taking it*) I am your moſt humble ſlave! Is it Hebe herſelf, or Venus in *la place* of Hebe? (*Amelia looks at him ſarcaſtically.*)

Baron. (*rather peeviſhly*) Neither Venus, nor Hebe, but Amelia Wildenhain with your permiſſion. But may I be informed of your loſs?

Count. Oh, my God! help me to baniſh the *triſte* remembrance, I am *envelopé* in a maze of perplexities. I am afraid I muſt even be obliged to write a letter upon the occaſion.

Baron. What? Is the misfortune really ſo great?

Count. (*ſipping his tea*) 'Tis abſolute nectar, moſt divine young lady! but could it be otherwiſe from your fair hands?

Baron. Indeed this nectar was ſold to me for plain congou tea.

Amelia. But, my good count, you do not tell us what you have loſt?

Baron. (*aſide*) His underſtanding!—

Count. You command—your ſlave obeys. But in doing this you tear open wounds, which even the ſight of

* The reader ſhould underſtand, that *fine gentlemen* in Germany as in England, affect to introduce phraſes of bad French into familiar converſation. T.

of you had ſcarcely healed. My *homme de chambre*—the *vaut-rien!*—Oh the man is a *mauvais ſujet.* As he was packing up my things the day before yeſterday, I ſaid to him, "*Henri*," ſaid I, "Yonder on that window ſtands a little pot of *pommade.*" You underſtand me, moſt charming lady, I ſaid to him moſt emphatically, "forget it not upon any conſideration, let it be packed up." I repeated it three times, nay, I believe, four times—"You know, *Henri*," I ſaid, "that I am undone without this *pommade*"—for you will underſtand, madam, they cannot make *pommade* here in Germany, they know not how to give it *l'odeur*—it is *incomparable.* I can aſſure you, madam, it comes *tout droit* from *Paris*, the author is *parfumeur du roi.* More than once, when I have been *dejour* * at her highneſs the princeſs *Adelaide*, ſhe has aſked, where I could get my *pommade*, "for count," ſhe ſaid, "the whole *chambre* is *parfumé* when you are with me *dejour.* Now only imagine, moſt charming lady, *et vous mon colonel*, the fellow totally forgot the *pommade*, there it ſtands upon the window ſtill, as I am a true *cavalier.*

Amelia. (*ſmiling*) Dreadful indeed!

Baron. Unleſs the mice ſhould have feaſted upon it.

Count. Et voila encore, mon colonel, another *raiſon* which drives me to deſperation. Would you believe it, this fellow, this *Henri*, has been thirty years in our ſervice! For thirty years has he been provided in our family with every thing for which a man of his *extraction* can have occaſion, and what does he now in return?—forgets my *pommade*—leaves it ſtanding on the window—as I am a *vrai cavalier.* *O Ciel!* and the German mice will perhaps gormandize upon the moſt delicate *parfum* that all France can produce. But it was impoſſible to reſtrain *mon indignation*; I inſtantly diſcharged him.

Baron. (*throwing himſelf back*) A ſervant who had lived with you thirty years!

Count. Oh be not uneaſy! I have another *in petto*—an excellent ſervant indeed! he dreſſes hair like a deity.

Amelia. And poor *Henri* muſt be turned away for ſuch a trifle!

* *Dejour* ſignifies the cuſtom which prevailed in France, of ladies being attended by gentlemen at their toilets. T.

Count. What ſay you, charming lady? a *Bagatelle?*

Amelia. Deprive a poor man of his bread!

Count. My God, how can I do leſs? Has he not deprived me of my *pommade?*

Amelia. May I not plead for him?

Count. Your ſentiments tranſport me! but your goodneſs muſt not be *abuſé.* The man has *quantité* of children, who in the courſe of time, when they are arrived at an *age mur* will be able to maintain their blockhead of a father.

Amelia. And has he a family too? Oh, I entreat you moſt earneſtly, count, not to diſcharge him!

Count. Vous etes aimable, divine creature!—*trés aimable!*—You command, your ſlave obeys. *Henri* ſhall come and kiſs the ſkirt of your garment.

Baron. (aſide, rubbing his hands impatiently) No! that is not to be borne!—away with the coxcomb! (*to the count*) What ſay you, count, to taking an hour's ſhooting before dinner?

Count. (kiſſing the ends of his fingers) Bravo! *mon colonel!* a *charmant* thought! I accept the party with pleaſure. *Madame*, you will then have a ſight of my elegant ſhooting-dreſs. You will find it in the very neweſt taſte. I had it made up on purpoſe *pour cette occaſion.* And my gun, *monſieur le colonel*, the ſtock is ſet with mother-of-pearl, you never ſaw any thing finiſhed with ſuperior *gout*; my arms are carved upon it.

Baron (drily) Can you ſhoot?

Count. I never was out a ſhooting but once in my life, and I cannot ſay then that I had the fortune to *attraper* any thing.

Baron. My gun is but an old and dull looking one to be ſure—but it brings down every bird at which 'tis aim'd.

Enter a Servant. The paſtor attends, ſir.

Baron. Well then, haſten, count, and put on your elegant ſhooting-dreſs, I will be with you quickly.

Count. I fly. My deareſt lady, it is *un ſacrifice* due to your father, thus to tear myſelf away for a while from his *aimable* daughter. (*Exit.*)

Baron. Hear me, Amelia!—It is ſcarcely neceſſary that I ſhould talk with the paſtor, and he afterwards talk with you. But ſtill, as he is here, leave us together—

 I have

I have other matters on which I wiſh to confer with him.

Amelia. (*going*) Dear father, I do not think I ever ſhall love the count.

Baron. As you pleaſe.

Amelia (*meeting the paſtor with a complacent ſmile*) Good morrow! good morrow! dear ſir. (*Exit.*)

SCENE VI. *The* BARON, *the* PASTOR.

Paſtor. I wait your lordſhip's commands.

Baron. Excuſe me if I have ſent for you at an inconvenient time, a few words will comprize my buſineſs—I yeſterday received a miſerable tranſlation from the French, which came from the preſs about twenty years ago. I myſelf poſſeſs a very elegant German original, of which, it is no vanity to ſay, that I am the author.—Now I am ſolicited to ſtrike my name out of the original, and bind it up together with this contemptible tranſlation—and I wiſh to aſk you, as corrector of my work, your opinion upon the ſubject.

Paſtor. Indeed, my lord, I do not underſtand your allegory.

Baron. No!——I am ſorry for that, I thought I had framed it ſo dexterouſly—but in ſhort then, the young Count von der Mulde is here, and would fain marry my daughter.

Paſtor. (*ſtarts but ſoon recovers himſelf*) Indeed!

Baron. He is a gentleman of the privy-chamber—but nothing elſe upon God's earth. He is—he is—in ſhort, I like him not.

Paſtor. (*rather eagerly*) And your daughter?

Baron. (*imitating her*) As you command—if you command—what you command—Well, well, but I think you know me ſufficiently to believe, that on ſuch an occaſion I would not lay any commands—yet, if the man's head were not ſo totally empty, and his heart were right, I ſhould have no objection; for his father is my old friend, and the match in other reſpects advantageous.

Paſtor. In other reſpects, my Lord?—what then remains to one, whoſe head and heart are good for nothing.

Baron. I only mean with reſpect to rank and fortune. My friend, I will explain to you my ideas upon this ſubject. If Amelia loved another, I ſhould not waſte a ſyllable upon the ſubject, I would only aſk who he is?—is all right here? *(pointing to his heart)*. If the anſwers were ſatisfactory, in God's name they ſhould have my bleſſing. But Amelia does not love any other man, which circumſtance alters the caſe entirely.

Paſtor. And never will love another.

Baron. Truly that is a different queſtion.—But underſtand me. I do not mean to perſiſt in this, I would only do what is incumbent on me not to offend the old Count von der Mulde, by refuſing to honour the bill of exchange, which he has drawn for my daughter; for I have already received the value in friendſhip from him; therefore I wiſh you to talk with my child, and explain to her the duties of the marriage ſtate, and this done, aſk her, whether ſhe be inclined to take upon herſelf thoſe duties as the wife of the young Count: if ſhe anſwer in the negative, 'tis enough---ſhe ſhall be urged no farther. What think you of this?

Paſtor. I—yes--certainly.—I underſtand you well--- I will talk with the young lady.

Baron. Yes, yes, do ſo! *(he fetches a deep ſigh)* Ah! one weight is now removed from my mind, but another hangs more heavily upon it, and oppreſſes it more grievouſly. You underſtand me—No ſucceſs yet, my friend? ſtill no intelligence?

Paſtor. I have ſought it with all diligence, but hitherto in vain.

Baron. Believe me, this has occaſioned me many a ſleepleſs night. How often is a man guilty of errors in his youth, which in age he would give all he poſſeſſes, could they be obliterated. How does he thus lay up a ſtore of miſery to corrode the happineſs of his future life, ſince the retroſpect of the paſt, and the hopes and proſpects of the future are inſeparably linked together. Is the view behind us darken'd o'er with clouds, ſo ſurely muſt we encounter ſtorms as we proceed onwards in our courſe. Well, well, we will hope the beſt. Farewell, my friend, I am going a ſhooting. In the mean time make your experiment, and remember to dine with me. [*Exit.*

Paſtor.

Paſtor. (alone) What a commiſſion!---to me? *(looking anxiouſly around)* If I ſhould meet with her directly!—No, I muſt firſt collect myſelf—prepare myſelf for the interview—at preſent it is impoſſible to encounter it.---A walk in the fields, and a devout prayer to heaven---then will I return---but ah, the *inſtructor* alone muſt come hither, the *man* I muſt leave at home. [*Exit.*

END OF THE SECOND ACT.

ACT

ACT III.

SCENE I. *An open Country.*

Enter FREDERICK *alone, holding ſome Pieces of Money in the Palm of his Hand.*

RETURN with theſe few pieces?—Return to ſee my mother die?---No, no, rather plunge into the water at once—rather run on to the end of the world. Ah, my feet ſeem clogged---I cannot advance—I cannot recede—the ſight of yonder ſtraw-roofed cottage, where reſts my ſuffering mother!—why muſt I always turn my eyes that way?—am I not ſurrounded by verdant fields and ſmiling meadows? why muſt my looks be ſtill drawn irreſiſtibly towards that cot which contains all my joys, all my ſorrows! *(looks with anguiſh at the money)* Man! man! is this your bounty? this piece was given me by the rider of a ſtately horſe followed by a ſervant, whoſe livery glittered with ſilver;—this, by a ſentimental lady who had alighted from her carriage to gaze at the country, deſcribe it, and print her deſcription. "Yon cottage," ſaid I to her, while my tears interrupted me—"It is very picturesque" ſhe anſwered, and ſkipped into her carriage. This was given me by a fat prieſt, enveloped in a large buſhy wig, who, at the ſame time, reviled me as an idler, a vagabond, and thus took away the merit of his gift. This *Dreyer (extremely affected)* a beggar gave me unaſked;---he ſhared with me his mite, and, at the ſame time, gave me God's bleſſing. Oh! at the awful day of retribution, how many fold will this dreyer be repaid by the all-righteous Judge! *(He pauſes and looks again at the money)* what can I purchaſe with this paltry ſum? Hardly will it pay for the nails of my poor mother's coffin---ſcarcely buy a rope

to

tò hang myſelf! *(He caſts a wiſhful look towards the diſtant country)* There inſultingly riſe the ſtately towers of the prince's reſidence;—ſhall I go thither? there implore pity?—Oh no! ſhe dwells not in cities—the cottage of the poor is her palace--the heart of the poor her Temple. Well then, ſhould a recruiting officer paſs by, for five rix-dollars paid on the ſpot, he ſhall have a ſtout and vigorous recruit. Five rix-dollars! Oh what a ſum! yet on how many a card may ſuch a ſum be ſtaked, even at this moment! *(wipes the ſweat from his forehead)* Father! Father! on thee fall theſe drops of anguiſh!—on thee the deſpair of a fellow creature, and all its dreadful conſequences!---yet God forbid that thou ſhouldſt languiſh in vain for pardon in another world, as my wretched mother languiſhes in this for a drop of wine. *(a hunting horn is heard at a diſtance,—a gun is fired,—ſucceeded by the "Halloo, Halloo," to the hounds; ſeveral dogs run over the ſtage, Frederick looks around)* Hunters! Noblemen probably! Well then, now to beg once more!—to beg for my mother!—Oh God! God! grant that I may meet with compaſſionate hearts!

SCENE II. *Enter the* BARON *and the* COUNT.

Baron. (Waiting a few moments for the Count who follows him out of breath) Quick, quick, Count!—Ha, ha!---that was a curſed blunder indeed—-the hounds have loſt the ſcent now and won't recover it again.

Count. (panting for breath) Tant mieux, tant mieux! mon colonel!—then one may take a little breath. *(ſupports himſelf on his gun. The Baron retires into the back ground and looks after the hounds;—Frederick advances with heſitation to the Count.)*

Fred. Noble Sir! I entreat alms of you!

Count. (*eyeing him from head to foot*) *Comment mon ami?* —-you are a damned impertinent fellow, you have limbs like *Hercule*,—your ſhoulders are equal to the Cretan Milo's;---I'll lay a wager you have ſtrength enough to carry an Ox.

Fred. If your lordſhip would permit me to make the experiment.

Count. Our police is not careful enough of idlers and vagabonds.

Fred.

Fred. (*with a ſignificant look*) So it appears to me! (*turns to the Baron who comes forward*) Noble Sir, have compaſſion on a wretched ſon who begs for a ſick mother!

Baron. (*puts his hand into his pocket and gives him a trifle*) It would be more proper, young man, to work for your ſick mother.

Fred. Willingly, willingly, would I work for her, but at this moment the neceſſity is too urgent—Pardon me, noble Sir, but what you have given me is not ſufficient?

Baron. (*ſurprized and miling*) Not ſufficient?

Fred. By God it is not!

Baron. This is ſingular! however, I ſhall give no more.

Fred. If you have any humanity give me a florin.

Baron. This is the firſt time that I ever heard a beggar preſcribe what I ſhould give him.

Fred. Oh, for heaven's ſake, noble Sir, give me a florin! you will reſcue a fellow-creature from deſpair!

Baron. You are beſide yourſelf, my friend.—Come along Count.

Count. *Allons, mon Colonel!*

Fred. For the love of God, my Lord, give a florin! You will ſave the lives of two unhappy wretches! (*as he ſees the Baron moving off he kneels to him*) a florin, noble Sir! you can never purchaſe the ſalvation of a man at a cheaper rate. (*The Baron moves onward, Frederick ruſhes wildly with his drawn ſword upon the Baron, and ſeizes him by the collar.*) Your money or your life.

Baron. (*agitated*) How! what! halloo! help! help! thieves! (*ſeveral huntſmen ruſh in and diſarm Frederick—the Count running off.*)

Fred. Oh God! what have I done!

Baron. Bear him away! take heed of him! confine him in the tower!—I ſhall follow immediately.

Fred. (*kneeling*) Only grant me one petition my Lord! I have forfeited my life, do with me what you will, but oh aſſiſt, I entreat you aſſiſt, my poor mother! ſhe languiſhes for want in yonder cottage—ſend thither and learn the truth! 'twas for my mother I drew my ſword, for her would I ſhed every drop of my blood.

Baron.

Baron. Away with him to the tower! keep him on bread and water.

Fred. (as he is borne off by the huntſmen) Accurſed be my father that he ever gave me exiſtence! [*Exeunt.*

Baron. (to another huntſman)) Francis—haſten to the village—If in the firſt, the ſecond, or the third houſe, you find a poor ſick woman, give her this purſe.

Huntſm. Very well, my Lord. [*Exit.*

Baron. Upon my ſoul this is a moſt extraordinary adventure! there is ſomething noble in the young fellow's countenance——ſhould it prove true that he begged for his mother—for his mother's ſake robbed upon the highway!—Well, well, we muſt inveſtigate the matter—this would indeed be a ſubject for one of Meiſſner's ſketches. [*Exit.*

SCENE III. *A Room in the* BARON's *Caſtle.*

Amelia. (alone) Why am I thus reſtleſs? What can be the matter with me?—I did not mean to come into this room—I meant to go into the garden. *(ſhe is going, but immediately returns.)* No, I will not go—Yes, but I think I will—I will ſee whether my auriculas are yet in flower, or whether the apple-kernels which our paſtor lately ſowed are come up.——Oh, they muſt be come up! (*returning again*) Then if any body ſhould come to ſpeak with me, I ſhall not be in the way, but muſt be called and ſought for.—No, better remain, here—yet the time will ſeem very tedious, *(ſhe pulls a noſegay to pieces)* Hark! did I not hear the houſe-door open? No, it was only the wind—I will look at my canary-birds. But ſuppoſe any body ſhould come, and not find me in the viſiting room? Yet who is likely to come? What makes my cheeks burn thus. *(She pauſes and begins to weep)* What have I to complain of? *(ſobbing)* why then ſhould I weep?

SCENE IV. *Enter the* PASTOR.

Amelia. (*cheers up and wipes her eyes)* Ah! good morning, dear Tutor!—Paſtor I would ſay—but you will pardon me, I have been ſo accuſtomed to call you Tutor.

Paſtor. Call me ſo ſtill, dear madam, I ſhall always hear it with pleaſure from your mouth.

Amelia. Indeed!

Paſtor. Yes, indeed!—Am I miſtaken? or have you not been weeping?

Amelia. Oh, 'tis nothing---a few tears only.

Paſtor. Yet they are tears—may one aſk what can have called them forth?

Amelia. I know not.

Paſtor. Perhaps thinking of your deceaſed mother?

Amelia. I might ſay yes---but——

Paſtor. A ſecret, perhaps—I would not be intruſive. ---Pardon me, madam, that I come hither at ſo unuſual an hour---I am commiſſioned by your Father.

Amelia. You are welcome to me at all times.

Paſtor. Indeed! am I really ſo?---Oh, Amelia——

Amelia. My father teaches me, that he who forms the heart and mind, is more one's benefactor, than he who merely gives one life *(caſting down her eyes)* my father ſays ſo, and my heart feels it.

Paſtor. How ſweetly does this moment repay me for eight years exertion.

Amelia. I was a wild girl---often have I ſeverely tried your patience—it is no more than juſt that I ſhould love you in return.

Paſtor. *(aſide)* Oh God! *(in a faultering, heſitating manner)* I—I—come from my Lord, your father---with a commiſſion—will you ſit down?

Amelia. *(fetches him a chair haſtily)* Sit down yourſelf —I had rather ſtand.

Paſtor. (*puſhing back the chair*) Count von der Mulde ---is come hither---

Amelia. Yes.

Paſtor. Do you know with what intention?

Amelia. To marry me.

Paſtor. That is indeed his wiſh (*very earneſtly*) But, believe me, madam, your father would on no account conſtrain you---no, he would by no means uſe compulſion.

Amelia. Ah, I know that well——

Paſtor. But he wiſhes—he deſires to aſcertain your inclination---I come to conſult your inclination——

Amelia. Towards the Count?

Paſtor.

Paſtor. Yes—no—rather on the ſubject of matrimony in general.

Amelia. What I am ignorant of, muſt be indifferent to me—I know nothing of the marriage ſtate.

Paſtor. For that very reaſon I wait upon you, madam, it is the ſubject of my commiſſion from your father. He wiſhes me to lay before you the agreeable and diſagreeable ſides of ſuch a condition.

Amelia. Begin then with the diſagreeable, the beſt ſhall be reſerved to the laſt.

Paſtor. With the diſagreeable?—Oh, madam, when two affectionate congenial hearts unite; the marriage ſtate has then no diſagreeable ſide. Hand in hand the happy pair journey through life. Where they find their path occaſionally ſtrewed o'er with thorns, diligently and cheerfully they clear their way. If a ſtream croſs their ſteps, the ſtronger bears the weaker over: or if a rock is to be climbed, the ſtronger takes the weaker by the hand:---patience and love are their companions. What would be impracticable *to one*, to their *united* efforts proves but ſport——and when they have reached the ſummit, the weaker wipes the ſweat from the brows of her more vigorous partner. Their joys their pains are never divided gueſts, nor can one ever experience a pang of ſorrow while tranſport warms the boſom of the other. A ſmile illumines the countenance of both; or tears diſtil from both their eyes. But their raptures are more lively and exſtatic than ſingle unparticipated joy; their ſorrow leſs corroding than ſolitary woe: for participation enhances the one, and alleviates the other. Thus their whole life reſembles a beautiful ſummer's day; beautiful, even though a tranſient ſhower may intervene:—for ſhowers refreſh the face of nature, and the ſun appears with added luſtre when it breaks out anew. And when the evening of their day draws on, it finds them ſurrounded with flowers, which they themſelves hv planted and reared, patiently awaiting the approach of night. Then, then, indeed——for night will come ——the one takes the lead and firſt lies down to ſleep, and happy *that* one, to whoſe lot it falls:——the ſurvivor wanders in melancholy ſolitude weeping at not being allowed to ſleep alſo.——And this is the only diſagreeable feature of ſuch a marriage.

Amelia. Oh, I will marry!

Pastor. Right, madam, this picture is alluring, but recollect that 'tis a picture for which two affectionate, congenial hearts sat as the models. But if motives of mere convenience (what the world generally terms prudence) if parental authority, rashness or caprice, tie the bonds of hymen, then, alas! the state of matrimony has *no* agreeable side. No longer free and unshackled man and woman walk with light and airy steps, but victims of a late repentance drag along their galling chains. Satiety is depicted on each brow. Images of lost happiness, painted in stronger colours by imagination's delusive hand, and more tempting in proportion as they are unattainable.—Sanguine and romantic hopes, which haply might never have been realized if this marriage had not taken place, but the practicability of which the mind holds certain, if the parties were not fettered by wedlock. These ideas incessantly harass the soul, and condemn them to actual suffering, where otherwise patience only would have been called into exertion. Gradually they accustom themselves to contemplate their irksome companion as the hateful cause of all the evils which befal them. Gall infuses itself into their conversation, coldness into their caresses. To none are they more captious, from none more apt to take offence, than from their wedded partner: and what would yield them delight in a stranger is viewed with apathy in the person of their nearest connection. In this manner, with averted face and downcast eyes, the hapless pair drag on through life, till at length one lies down to sleep:——then exultingly the survivor lifts the head and triumphantly exclaims, "Liberty! Liberty!"—And this forms the *only* pleasing feature in such a marriage.

Amelia. I will not marry!

Pastor. That is in other words to say I will not love.

Amelia. Ha!—yes—I will marry—for I will love—I love already.

Pastor. (*extremely confused*) Indeed!—You love the Count von der Mulde?

Amelia. Oh no! no!—away with the fool (*taking both his hands with the most cordial familiarity*) I love you.

Pastor. Madam, for God's sake!

Amelia.

Amelia. And you will I marry.

Paſtor. Me!

Amelia. Yes, you, dear tutor.

Paſtor. Amelia!—you forget——

Amelia. What do I forget?

Paſtor. That you are of noble extraction.

Amelia. What ſignifies that?

Paſtor. Oh, Heavens!—No, that cannot be.

Amelia. If you have an affection for me?

Paſtor. I love you as my life.

Amelia. Well, then, marry me.

Paſtor. Oh, ſpare me, Amelia!—I am a miniſter of religion, 'tis true—that gives me much fortitude—but ſtill I am a man.

Amelia. You have yourſelf exhibited to me ſo alluring a picture of the marriage ſtate!—But I am not, then, the woman with whom you could go hand in hand, with whom you could ſhare all your joys, all your ſorrows?

Paſtor. Were it in my choice, you only ſhould be the perſon. Did we live in the golden days of which poets dream, when all ranks were equal, I would have you alone. But 'tis not for us to alter the cuſtoms of the world; and as the world is now conſtituted, you muſt marry a man of rank.——Whether you would be happy or not with the humble paſtor, is not the queſtion.——Oh, God! I have already ſaid too much!

Amelia. Others, perhaps, may not make that a queſtion, but it muſt be one with me.—Have you not often told me that the heart alone ennobles us. (*She places her hand upon his heart*) Oh, truly, I ſhall marry a *nobleman.*

Paſtor. Madam! let me entreat you to call in reaſon to your aid.—A thouſand objections lie againſt ſuch an union—but, at this moment, Heaven knows, not one occurs to me.

Amelia. Becauſe in truth there are none.

Paſtor. Yet, yet—but my heart is ſo full—my heart would plead—but that it ſhall not, muſt not. Think only of the ſneers of your relations—how they will ſhun you, aſhamed of the new connection you have brought among them—on thoſe ſolemn days when all the family ſhould be collected together, omitting to invite you, ſhaking their heads when your name is mentioned,

tioned, whiſpering your ſtory, forbidding their children to play with yours, or even to accoſt them with familiarity——embroidering their arms upon their liveries, painting them upon their carriages, while you muſt ride in one humble and unornamented---ſcarcely recollecting you, ſhould they meet you at a third place—or, if they ſhould condeſcend to favour you with a word, addreſſing you not as a lady of rank, but with ſcornful countenances, as the parſon's wife.——

Amelia. Ha! ha! ha! Is that ſo very terrible?

Paſtor. You laugh?

Amelia. Yes; you muſt pardon me, dear tutor. For eight years was I under your inſtruction, but in all that time never were any of your precepts advanced upon ſuch ſhallow reaſonings as thoſe you have now uttered.

Paſtor. I am ſorry for that---extremely ſorry, indeed! for——

Amelia. It rejoices me extremely---for——

Paſtor. (*much embarraſſed*) For——

Amelia. For—you muſt marry me.

Paſtor. Never!

Amelia. You know me well---you know that I am not untractable, and from a conſtant intercourſe with you, I ſhall daily improve. I will take all poſſible pains to make you happy---or rather, it ſhall coſt me no pains to make you ſo. Together we will live, happy, truly happy in each other, till one of us lie down to ſleep, and then the other ſhall weep, indeed; but that time be yet far diſtant. Well, then, conſent, elſe ſhall I think you have no regard for me.

Paſtor. Oh! it is glorious to maintain the character of a man of honour; but the taſk is often hard. Madam, did you but know how much you torture me!——No, no, this muſt not, cannot be! I ſhould ſink into the earth at the moment, were I to attempt to make ſuch a propoſal to your father.

Amelia. I will make it myſelf.

Paſtor. For Heaven's ſake, forbear! To his liberality I owe my preſent comfortable ſituation---to his friendſhip the happieſt hours of my life---and ſhall I, ungrateful wretch! miſlead his daughter, his only child!——Oh, God! Oh, God! thou ſeeſt the purity of my intentions! ſupport me in this conflict!

Amelia. My father wiſhes me to marry—he wiſhes to ſee me happy. Well then, I will marry. I will be happy—but with you only. Thus will I tell my father, and what will be his anſwer.—At the firſt moment he will ſtart, and ſay, "Girl, art thou mad!" but ſoon he will recollect himſelf, and, ſmiling, add, "Well, well, in God's name be it ſo." Then will I kiſs his hand, ſkip away from him, and fly into your arms. It ſhall be told about that I am betrothed; the country people, with their wives, from the whole village, will come and wiſh me joy, and aſk God's bleſſing upon us both—and God will bleſs us.—Certainly, certainly, he will bleſs us.—Ah! ever ſince my father returned hither, I have not known what it was ſo oppreſſed my heart, but I know it now—it is now lightened. *(taking his hand.)*

Paſtor. (*withdrawing his hand.*) Oh! you have almoſt deprived me of my ſenſes—and of more, of my peace of mind.

Amelia. No, no.—But I hear ſome one on the ſtairs—I have yet many things to ſay to you.

SCENE V. *Enter* CHRISTIAN *the Butler, an old Servant in the Houſe.*

Amelia. (*peeviſhly.*) Ah! is it you?

Chriſt. Without vanity be it ſpoken, Chriſtian Lebrecht Goldmann has purſued his way hither the moment the happy news reached his ears.

Amelia. (embarraſſed) What news?

Paſtor. (confuſed) He has overheard us!

Chriſt. A faithful, old ſervant, young lady, who has often carried the lady your mother in his arms, and, without vanity be it ſpoken, has received from her many a box on the ear, hath, on this joyful day, flown hither to preſent his humble gratulations.——Sing, Oh, Muſe! on the happy occaſion—ſtrike up thy notes, Oh Lyre!

Amelia. My good Chriſtian, I have no inclination at preſent to attend to your muſe or to your lyre. And what is the matter now?

Chriſt. Ah! my noble, bleſſed young lady—
To-day I cannot ſilent be,
But hither muſt command to flee

Trumpet,

Trumpet, violin, and drum,
As faſt as ever they can come;
And bid my verſes ſoftly flow,
As waters through the meadows go.

Hitherto has no birth-day, or wedding-day, or chriſtening-day, or their anniverſaries, been ſolemnized in the moſt noble Baron's family, which has not been celebrated by an offering from my ever-ready and obedient muſe. In the courſe of ſix-and-forty years, no leſs than three hundred ninety and ſeven congratulatory effuſions have flowed from my pen. To-day, the three hundred ninety and eighth ſhall echo around. Who knows how ſoon a ſolemn marriage affiance in Chriſt may furniſh an opportunity for a three hundred ninety and ninth !——and then, ha ! ha ! ha !—in another year will come the four hundredth.

Amelia. To-day is Friday—that is the only thing remarkable in it, that I can recollect.

Chriſt. Yes, indeed, it is Friday; but more—in the firſt place, Heaven has been pleaſed to reſcue our noble lord the Baron from an imminent danger—and in the ſecond place, it is therefore a day of rejoicing.

Amelia. Reſcued my father from danger !—What do you mean?

Chriſt. This very moment has the huntſman Frank arrived in haſte, and advertiſed the congregated houſehold of his lordſhip of a piece of villainy, which the lateſt poſterity, without vanity be it ſpoken, never ſhall read without the ſtrongeſt emotions of horror.

Amelia. (anxiouſly) Oh! tell it me quickly.

Chriſt. Our moſt noble Baron, and the foreign Count of the Holy Roman Empire, had ſcarcely

One half hour trodden the unbeaten way,
To ſeek the nimble-footed hare to ſlay.

Amelia. For heavens ſake tell it me in proſe!

Chriſt. My Lord Baron had already ſhot one hare—for I myſelf have had the honour of ſeeing it; the left fore foot was quite torn to pieces.

Amelia. (*impatiently*) Well, well, but my father!

Chriſt. A ſecond hare was already ſtarted, and the hounds purſued her with due activity, particularly Spadillio, he more than any other diſtinguiſhed himſelf, when ſuddenly his honourable Lordſhip was met in the midſt of the field by a ſoldier who demanded alms. Frank, the huntſman himſelf, ſaw how the moſt noble Baron with inexpreſſible kindneſs felt in his pocket, drew out a piece of money, and gave it to the beggar. But the ungrateful, audacious, high-way robber, ſuddenly drew his ſword, fell, without vanity be it ſpoken, like a mad dog upon his honourable Lordſhip, and had not our active huntſmen haſtened in a moment to his aſſiſtance, I, poor old man, ſhould have been under the mournful neceſſity of compoſing a funeral elegy, and an epitaph in commemoration of his melancholy exit.

Amelia. (*terrified*) My God!

Paſtor. A highway-robber!---in broad day-light!---that is extraordinary!

Chriſt. I muſt form it into a ballad after the manner of Bürger.

Paſtor. Is not the man taken up?

Chriſt. Yes, indeed he is. The moſt noble Baron has commanded, that till further orders, he be confined in the old Tower. Frank ſays he will be here immediately: (*he ſteps to the window*) I believe, indeed—the ſun blinds me a little---they are coming already---Sing Oh muſe, ſtrike up thy notes Oh lyre! (*he runs out, the others go to the window*).

Amelia. Never in my life did I ſee a highway robber!—he muſt doubtleſs have a terrifying phyſiognomy.

Paſtor. Did you never ſee the Female Parricide in Lavater's Fragments?

Amelia. A female Parricide!—Can ſuch a monſter exiſt in the world?—But look—the young ſoldier approaches—an intereſting figure indeed!---a noble countenance!---yet it is full of ſorrow!—the poor man excites my compaſſion.—No, no; he cannot be a highway robber!---Oh, fye, fye! ſee how the huntſmen thruſt him into the Tower! hard-hearted wretches!---now they lock the door---and now he is in total darkneſs—what muſt be the feelings of the unhappy creature!

Paſtor. (*aſide*) They can ſcarcely be more poignant than mine.

SCENE VI. *Enter the* BARON.

Amelia. (*running up to him*) A thouſand congratulations to you, dear father!

Baron. For God's ſake ſpare me!---Old Chriſtian has been pouring out his congratulations in Alexandrines all the way up ſtairs.

Paſtor. The ſtory then is true?---indeed, as related by the talkative old Butler, it appeared wholly incredible.

Amelia. The young man with the intereſting countenance was, indeed, a highway robber?

Baron. 'Tis true; yet am I almoſt convinced that he was ſo for the firſt and laſt time in his life. My friend, (*to the paſtor*) it was a moſt ſingular accident.-----He begged of me for his mother.---I gave him a trifle---I might, perhaps, have given him more, but the hares were running in my head, and the cry of the hounds filled my ears. You know well, that when a man purſues his pleaſure, he has no feeling for the afflictions of his brethren. In ſhort, he wanted more---deſpair was in his whole manner, yet I turned my back upon him; loſt to himſelf he drew his ſword, but I would wager my life againſt Amelia's head-dreſs, that highway-robbing is not his trade.

Amelia. Certainly not.

Baron. He trembled as he held me by the breaſt, a child might have knocked him down. Oh, it was a ſhame that I did not ſuffer the poor wretch to eſcape. My ſport may perhaps coſt him his life, and I might have ſaved it---ſaved the life of a man for a florin only. Ah, that he had not been ſeen by my people! but the bad example!---come with me to my cloſet, good Paſtor, we muſt contrive how we can beſt ſave the culprit; for ſhould he be conſigned over to the arm of juſtice, adieu to all hopes of deliverance. (*going.*)

Amelia. Dear father, I have had much converſation with the Paſtor.

Baron. Have you?---and on the ſubject of the holy marriage ſtate?

Amelia. Yes; I have told him---

Paſtor. (*extremely embarraſſed*) In conſequence of my commiſſion------

Amelia. He will not believe me—

Paſtor. I have explained to the young lady——

Amelia. And indeed I ſpoke from my heart——

Paſtor. (*pointing to the cloſet*) May I requeſt——

Amelia. But his diffidence———

Paſtor. The reſult of our converſation ſhall be related in your cloſet——

Baron. What the devil is the matter now;—you interrupt each other, ſo that neither can go on. Amelia, have you entirely forgotten all the rules of politeneſs?

Amelia. Oh, no, dear father!---but is it not true that you ſaid you would let me marry whom I ſhould chuſe?

Baron. Aſſuredly!

Amelia. Hear you not, dear Tutor?

Paſtor. (*takes out his handkerchief in haſte, and holds it to his face*) I beg your pardon, my Lord, I am not well. [*Exit.*

Baron. (*calls after him*) I ſhall expect you! (*Going.*)

Amelia. Stop a moment, dear father! I have moſt important things to communicate.

Baron. (*ſmiling*) Important things! I ſuppoſe you want me to buy you a new fan. [*Exit.*

Amelia. (*alone*) A fan!—indeed I think I am in want of a fan, (*ſhe fans herſelf with her pocket-handkerchief*) my cheeks burn ſo; but this will not relieve me! Ah my God how my heart beats!---I do, indeed I do, moſt dearly love the Paſtor; how unfortunate that he ſhould be taken ill juſt now;---No, the Count ſcarcely deſerves the name of man. When I contemplate my father or the Paſtor, I feel a ſort of reverence; but the Count I feel only diſpoſed to ridicule. (*ſhe goes to the window*) The tower is ſtill locked. Oh how terrible muſt be ſuch confinement!---I wonder whether the poor man has any thing to eat and drink! (*ſhe beckons and calls*) Chriſtian! Chriſtian! come hither directly!---the young man intereſts me—I know not why, but he does intereſt me: he has hazarded his life for his mother, that does not beſpeak a bad heart.

SCENE

SCENE VII. *Enter* CHRISTIAN.

Amelia. Ah, good Chriſtian, tell me, have you carried the priſoner any thing to eat?

Chriſt. Yes, my moſt benevolent young lady!

Amelia. What have you carried him?

Chriſt. Good black bread, and fine clear water.

Amelia. Oh fye!---are you not aſhamed?—haſten inſtantly into the kitchen and get ſome meat from the cook, then fetch a bottle of wine from the cellar, and carry them to him immediately.

Chriſt. Moſt gladly would I fulfil the will of my moſt benevolent young lady, but at preſent he muſt be content with bread and water, for the moſt noble lord baron hath expreſsly commanded——

Amelia. Ah, my father only did that in the firſt moments of paſſion.

Chriſt. What our noble maſters command in paſſion, 'tis the duty of a faithful old ſervant, without vanity be it ſpoken, to obey in cold blood.

Amelia. You are a great oaf!---ſo old, and have not yet learnt that 'tis your duty to comfort the unfortunate. Give me the key of the cellar, I will go myſelf.

Chriſt I ſolemnly proteſt moſt bleſſed Lady——

Amelia. Give it to me, I command you.

Chriſt. *(gives her the key)* I muſt go immediately, and exculpate myſelf to his honourable Lordſhip.

Amelia. You may do that with all my heart.

[*Exit haſtily.*

Chriſt. *(after a pauſe, and ſhaking his head.)*

In woe and anguiſh,
Each day to languiſh,
Is right affecting
And dejecting.
Is then the youthful mind
To follow good inclin'd;
Let him ſtill in memory keep
The good old proverb, look before you leap.

[*Exit.*

END OF THE THIRD ACT.

ACT IV.

SCENE I. *A Priſon in an old Tower in the Caſtle of Wildenhain.*

FREDERICK (*alone*).

HOW can a few moments of anguiſh—one hour of devouring miſery ſwallow up all the paſt happineſs of a man's life! When I left the inn this morning, the ſun was juſt riſing, I ſang my morning ſong, and oh how cheerful, how happy was I!—In thought I banqueted at the table of joy,—I dreamt with tranſport of the firſt re-union with my mother!—I meant to ſteal along the road towards the ſpot where ſhe once dwelt; thought how I ſhould creep cloſe by the wall, that ſhe might not from the window eſpy my approach; and when arrived at the houſe-door, how I ſhould ſoftly, ſoftly pull the bell.—Then in idea, I ſaw her lay aſide her work, riſe up, and come down, I thought how my heart would beat, when I ſhould hear her ſteps upon the ſtairs, how ſhe would open the door to me, and I ſhould throw myſelf into her arms. But oh, farewell, ye air-built caſtles, ye beauteous variegated bubbles, ſeen through hope's priſmatic glaſs!—I returned to my native land, and the firſt object which met my eyes was my dying mother, my firſt habitation is a priſon, and my firſt going forth will be to the place of execution. Oh righteous God! have I deſerved this fate? or muſt the ſon anſwer for the crimes of a father! But be ſtill, my heart—I entangle myſelf in a labyrinth! To ſuffer without murmuring, to ſorrow and be ſilent! Such is the leſſon taught me by my mother, and ſhe hath ſuffered much!—Thou, oh God, thou art juſt! (*looks towards Heaven with uplifted hands*)

SCENE II. *Enter* AMELIA *with a plate of proviſions and a bottle of wine.*

Fred. (*turning round at the noiſe*) Who's there?

Amelia. My good friend, I bring you ſome refreſhment—you may perhaps be hungry or thirſty.

Fred. Alas no! I feel neither hunger nor thirſt.

Amelia. Here is a bottle of old wine, and ſome meat.

Fred. (*eagerly*) Old wine! really, good old wine?

Amelia. I do not underſtand much of wine myſelf, but I have often heard my father ſay this wine is a true cordial.

Fred. Ten thouſand, thouſand thanks, lovely, amiable, Unknown! You make me a coſtly preſent indeed, in this bottle of wine.—Oh haſten, haſten then, moſt benevolent tender-hearted maiden, let it be inſtantly diſpatched to the neighbouring village; cloſe by the public-houſe ſtands a little cottage, where will be found a poor, ſick woman—a fainting woman, whom, if ſhe yet live, this wine may revive! (*he takes the bottle from Amelia's hand, and raiſes it up towards heaven*) Oh God! bleſs this liquor! why can I not myſelf?—(*gives back the bottle to Amelia*) but no—haſten, haſten then with it, moſt amiable of your ſex! ſave my mother, and you will be my guardian angel.

Amelia. (*much affected*) Worthy creature! Oh I am right, he cannot be a villain, a murderer!

Fred. God be thanked, that I ſtill deſerve to be noticed by ſo noble a ſoul!

Amelia. I will go myſelf immediately.—But let me leave this bottle of wine here; I will fetch another for your poor mother. (*ſhe ſets down the bottle and is going*)

Fred. Yet one word more. Let me know, ſweet maiden, who you are, that in my prayers to heaven, your name may be remembered.

Amelia. My father is Baron Wildenhain, the poſſeſſor of this eſtate.

Fred. Merciful God!!!—

Amelia. What is the matter?

Fred. (*ſhuddering*) And the man, againſt whom I this day drew my ſword!

Amelia. Was my father?

Fred. My FATHER!!!

Amelia. I feel agitated in his preſence. (*She runs out.*)

SCENE III. FREDERICK. (*Alone.*)

(*He repeats the words with agony.*) Was my FATHER! —Eternal

—Eternal juſtice thou ſlumbereſt not!—The man againſt whom I drew my ſword this day—was my FATHER!—A few moments more, and I had been a parricide!—Oh—h—h! an icy coldneſs freezes all my limbs—my hair ſtands an end—a miſt floats before my ſight—Oh for breath! for breath! (*he ſinks down on his ſeat—a long pauſe.*) What a tumult does this idea raiſe in my brain!—how the horrid images flit before my eyes as clouds and vapours, which every moment change their forms.—And if fate had deſtined him thus to be ſacrificed!—had my arm conſummated the dreadful ſtroke!—Great Judge of all things, whoſe had been the guilt?—Would not thyſelf have armed the hand of the ſon, to avenge a mother's wrongs on an unnatural father?—* Oh Zadig! Zadig!—(*he is loſt for ſome minutes in deep reflection*)—but this maiden—this amiable, lovely, inexpreſſibly lovely creature,—who has juſt left me,—who has awakened a new and moſt tranſporting ſenſation in my breaſt,—this lovely creature is my ſiſter!—And the ſilly being, the coxcomb, who accompanied my father, was he then my brother?—an ill-educated boy, who as it appears to me, from his youth conſidered as the only heir, has been taught to regard nothing but his wealth, his rank, and is thus inflated with his own conſequence, while I, his brother, and my dear mother, ſuffer want.

SCENE IV. *Enter* PASTOR.

Paſtor. God preſerve you, my friend!

Fred. And you too, Sir. Judging by your appearance, you are of the church; therefore a meſſenger of peace. You are truly welcome to me.

Paſtor. I wiſh to bring peace and tranquillity to your ſoul. Reproaches I ſhall ſpare, for your own conſcience muſt upbraid you more loudly than the preacher's voice.

Fred. Oh, you are right!——And, where conſcience then is ſilent, are you not of opinion, that the crime at leaſt is doubtful?

Paſtor. Or muſt have been perpetrated by a wicked and obdurate heart indeed.

* Referring to Voltaire's well-known novel of "*Zadig, or the Book of Fate.*" T.

Fred.

Fred. That is not my cafe. I really would not change this heart for that of any prince—no, nor any prieft.—Pardon me, Sir, that was not aimed at you.

Paſtor. And if it was, mildneſs is the character of the religion, I teach.

Fred. I only mean to ſay—that my heart is not obdurate, yet my conſcience does not reproach me with a crime.

Paſtor. Does it not deceive you?—Self-love ſometimes uſurps the place of conſcience.

Fred. No! no!—Oh, tis a pity that I am not more endued with learning,—that I underſtand not in what way properly to arrange my ideas,—that I can only feel—that I cannot demonſtrate!—Yet, let me aſk you, Sir, what was my crime?—that I would have robbed!—Oh, for a few moments put yourſelf in my place:—have you any parents?

Paſtor. No, I was early left an orphan.

Fred. Pity!—pity indeed! then you cannot fairly judge me.—Yet will I deſcribe my caſe as well as I am able. I think, when one looks around, and ſees how nature every where exuberantly pours forth her ample ſtores; when one obſerves this ſpectacle, and beholds at the ſame time a dying mother by one's ſide, who with parched tongue faints for a drop of wine—if then one rich, and bleſſed with abundance, ſhould paſs by, and ſhould deny the deſpairing wretch a florin, becauſe—becauſe it would interrupt his ſport—then ſuddenly the feelings of the equality of all mankind ſhould be awakened in the ſufferer's ſoul, and ſeeing himſelf neglected by fortune, he ſhould determine to reſume his rights—rights authorized by nature, who is not unjuſt to any of her children; and ſhould inſtinctively graſp at a ſmall ſhare of thoſe bounties which ſhe preſents to all—Such a man does not plunder, he rightly takes his own.

Paſtor. My friend, were theſe principles univerſal, they would cut aſunder every tie that binds ſociety, and change us ſoon into Arabian hordes.

Fred. 'Tis poſſible! and 'tis alſo poſſible, that we ſhould not be more unhappy.—Among the hoſpitable Arabs my Mother would not have been ſuffered to ſtarve on the highway!

Paſtor. (*Much ſurpriſed*) Young man, you appear to have had an education above your rank.

Fred. That is foreign to the purpofe—for what I am, I am indebted to my mother.—I would only reprefent to you, why my confcience does not accufe me.—The judge pronounces fentence according to the letter of the law, the Divine fhould judge not merely the deed itfelf, but the motive which prompted it. The Judge might then condemn me, but you, oh Sir, would inftantly pronounce my pardon.—That the glutton, who picks even the laft morfel from his pheafant's bones, fhould leave unmolefted his neighbour's black bread, can be no merit.

Paftor. Well, young man! fuppofe I grant your fophifm; grant, that perhaps your peculiar fituation allowed you to *take*, what you could not obtain by folicitation, does that alfo exculpate murder, which you meditated.

Fred. Murder! no, it does not exculpate that. Still I was but the inftrument of a higher power. In this adventure, you only behold one folitary link of a mighty chain, held by an invifible hand, On this fubject I cannot explain, cannot juftify myfelf. Yet, fhall I appear with ferenity before my judge, with calmnefs meet my death, convinced that an all-powerful hand intends by my blood, the accomplifhment of fome great purpofe in the career of fate.

Paftor. It is well worth fome pains, moft extraordinary young man, to be better acquainted with you, and perhaps to give a different complexion to many of your ideas. If it be poffible, continue with me for fome weeks, and give me your confidence. Your fick mother I will alfo take to my houfe.

Fred. (*embraces him*) A thoufand thanks for my poor mother's fake. As for myfelf, you know that I am a prifoner, in expectation of receiving fentence of death. The refpite which the forms of juftice may afford, ufe at your pleafure.

Paftor. You are miftaken.—You are in the hands of a noble-minded man, who honours your filial love, compaffionates your unhappy fituation, and heartily forgives you what has this day happened. You are free—He fent me hither to announce to you your liberty, and with a paternal exhortation, a brotherly admonition, to releafe you from your prifon.

Fred. And the name of this generous man?

Paftor. Is the Baron von Wildenhain.

Fred.

Fred. Von Wildenhain! (*as if he was recollecting himself*) Did he not live formerly in Franconia*?

Pastor. You are right. But at the death of his Lady, a few weeks since, he returned to this, his paternal estate.

Fred. His wife then is dead?—and that amiable girl, who was here just before your arrival, is his daughter?

Pastor. Yes, she is his daughter, the Lady Amelia.

Fred. And the *perfumed* young man is his son?

Pastor. He has no son.

Fred. (*eagerly*) Yes he has! (*recollecting himself*) I mean the young man who was sporting with him to-day.

Pastor. No, he is not his son.

Fred. (*aside*) God be thanked!

Pastor. Only a visitor from town.

Fred. I thank you for this information; it is highly interesting to me. I also thank you for the kind trouble you have taken, the philanthropy you have shewn. It grieves me that I cannot offer you my friendship—were we equals it might be of some value.

Pastor. Has not friendship this property in common with love, that it equalizes all ranks?

Fred. No, kind Pastor, this enchantment is peculiar to love alone!—Yet I have one more request to make—Conduct me to the Baron von Wildenhain, and procure me, if it be in your power, a few minutes conversation with him in private; I wish to thank him for his benevolence, but if any one be with him, I should be confused, and could not speak with so much confidence.

Pastor. Follow me. [*Exeunt.*

SCENE V. *A room in the Castle.*

The BARON *seated on a chair, and smoking his pipe—* AMELIA *in conversation with him—The* COUNT *upon the Sopha, one moment taking snuff, another holding a smelling-bottle to his nose.*

Baron. No, no, my child, let it alone at present—to-

* In the performance, Alsace and France, are throughout used instead of Franconia; no reason for this appears. It was probably a mistake arising from the substantive *Franken*, i. e. Franconia, being applied in modern language to *French* as an adjective, instead of *Franzosen*. T.

wards

wards evening, when it grows cool, we may take a walk that way.

Amelia. It is fo delightful to do a good action!—why then fhould one depute it to a fervant? To confer a kindnefs is a real joy, and no one is of too high rank for enjoyment.

Baron. Simpleton, who fpoke of rank? That was a filly remark which almoft makes me angry. I tell you I have fent to the cottage myfelf, the woman is better; and in the evening we will take a walk thither together. The Paftor fhall conduct us.

Amelia. (*tolerably fatisfied*) Well, as you pleafe. (*fhe fits down and takes out her work*)

Baron. (*to the Count*) It will be a great pleafure to you alfo, Count.

Count. *Je n'en doute pas, mon Colonel*, the *douceur* and the *bonté d'ame of Mademoifelle* will charm me. But what if the good woman fhould have gotten fome epidemical difeafe? However I have a *vinaigre incomparable* againft the plague,—we will at leaft be prepared with that.

Baron. As you pleafe, Count. I do not know any better prefervative to offer you againft *ennui*, than fuch a cordial.

Count. *Ennui*, oh *mon Colonel!* Who can think of *ennui* in the fame houfe with *Mademoifelle?*

Baron. Very gallantly fpoken!—Amelia, don't you thank the Count?

Amelia. I thank him, truly. (*the Count makes a complimentary bow*).

Baron. Tell me, Count, did you refide long in France?

Count. Oh talk not to me of France, I entreat you, *mon Colonel*—you rend my heart.—My father, *le barbare*, had the *fottife* to refufe me a thoufand Louis-d'ors which I had *deftiné* for that purpofe. It is true I was there fome months—I have indeed feen that dear place replete with charms, and, fpite of *le barbare de pere*, I had perhaps been there ftill, but for a moft unpleafant occurrence.

Baron. (*fneeringly*) Probably *une affaire d'honneur.*

Count. *Point du tout* but it was no longer a place in which a *vrai Cavalier* could remain with credit to himfelf. You have heard of the Revolution? Oh yes, you muft have heard of it, for it is the converfation of all Europe. —*Eh bien! imaginez vous!*—I was at Paris, I went into the

the *Palais Royal*, I knew nothing at all of what was paſſing—*tout d'un coup* I perceived myſelf ſurrounded by a crowd of dirty raggamuffins, one kicked me on one ſide, another puſhed me on the other ſide, another thruſt his fiſts in my face.—I aſked what was the meaning of all this? They abuſed me, and cried that I had no cockade in my hat—you underſtand me, no national cockade. I ſcreamed out that I was *Comte du Saint Empire.*—What did they do?—they abſolutely caned me—*foi d'honnete homme* they caned me, and a dirty *Poiſſarde* gave me a filip on the noſe;—indeed there were even ſome who would have had me *à la lanterne.*—What ſay you to this? what would you have done *à ma place?* I threw myſelf with all poſſible expedition into my poſt-chaiſe, and haſtened away with all poſſible ſpeed.—*voila tout!* it is indeed *une hiſtoire facheuſe*, but nevertheleſs I muſt ever regret the *moments delicieuſes* which I have taſted in that *capitale du monde*, and this I muſt ſay, this muſt every one perceive, that though indeed, I paſſed but a few months there, *mon ſavoir vivre*, *mon formation*, and, *le plie*, which is obſerved in me, are perfectly *Françoiſe*, perfectly *Pariſien.*

Baron. Of that I am no judge, but your language does not appear to me German.

Count. Ah, *mon Colonel*, you pay me a high compliment.

Baron. I am glad you take it as ſuch.

Count. Then all my *ſoins* have happily not been taken *à pure perte.* For five years paſt have I made every poſſible effort totally and completely to forget German. What ſay you, Madam, is not the German language entirely devoid of grace, and at beſt, only *ſupportable* in ſo lovely a mouth as yours. That eternal guggling and rattling in the throat—*a tout moment*—one reels—one ſtumbles—it does not flow, roll, ſmoothly on—as *par exemple*, one would make a *declaration d'amour*, one wiſhes it to be a *chef d'œuvre d'eloquence.* Well, one ſtudies it, but, *helas*, ſcarcely has one gone through a *douzaine* of words, but the tongue hitches now here, now there; thruſts itſelf firſt one way, then the other; the teeth run *péle méle* againſt one another; the throat quarrels with the roof of the mouth, and if one did not throw in a few French words to ſet all to rights again, one ſhould run the hazard of loſing, irrecoverably, the faculties of ſpeech. *Et convenez vous à cela Mademoiſelle*, that this cannot be otherwiſe

otherwise—for why? we have no *genies celèbres*, whose taste is properly refined. I know, indeed, that at present the Germans pique themselves much, *sur la gout*, *la lecture*, *les belles lettres*. There is a certain Monsieur Wieland, who has gained some *renommeé*, by translating some tales from the *Mille et une nuits*, but *mon dieu*, still the original is French.

Baron. But what the devil is the matter, Count, that you are every moment snuffing up your *tabac*, or holding your smelling-bottle to your nose, and drenching your clothes and my sopha with *Eau de Lavande*, and making the air in my room so *fade*, that it is like the shop of a French *Marchand des modes*.

Count. *Pardonnez*, *mon Colonel*, but it must be confessed that the smoke of your tobacco is altogether *insupportable*—my nerves are most sensibly affected with it—my clothes must be hung a month at least in the open air to purify them—and I assure you, *mon Colonel*, it even gives a taint to the hair. It is a vile custom, which indeed one must pardon in *Messieurs du Militaire*, because *en campagne*, they have no opportunity of mixing with the *beau monde*, and acquiring the manners of *ton*. But at present, there is no possibility of enduring this *horrible* smell any longer.—*Vous m'excuserez*, *mon Colonel*—but I must go and breathe a little fresh air, and change my clothes. [*Exit.*

SCENE VI. *The* BARON *and* AMELIA.

Baron. Bravo, my young gentleman!—I know, now, however, a means of getting rid of you, when I am tired of your twattling.

Amelia. Dear father, I cannot take him for a husband.

Baron. Dear child, I cannot take him for a son.

Amelia. (*Who appears to have something on her mind.*) I cannot endure him.

Baron. Nor I neither.

Amelia. What can one do, if one cannot bear the man?

Baron. Nothing at all.

Amelia. Love comes and goes unsolicited.

Baron. It does so indeed.

Amelia. It is often scarcely possible to give a reason why one loves or hates.

Baron. That may be the cafe.

Amelia. Yet there are cafes in which one's inclination, or averfion, are founded upon good grounds.

Baron. Undoubtedly.

Amelia. For example, my averfion to the Count.

Baron. Certainly.

Amelia. And my inclination towards the Paftor.

Baron. Yes. *(Both paufe.)*

Amelia. Probably I may marry.

Baron. And you ought to marry. *(Both paufe again.)*

Amelia. Why does not our Paftor marry?

Baron. That you muft afk him himfelf. *(Paufe again.)*

Amelia. *(She keeps her eyes conftantly on her work, at which fhe is very bufily employed.)* He feems to have a great regard for me.

Baron. I am glad to hear it.

Amelia. And I have alfo a great regard for him.

Baron. That is but juft. *(Another paufe.)*

Amelia. I believe if you were to offer him my hand, he would not refufe it.

Baron. I believe fo myfelf.

Amelia. And I would readily obey you.

Baron. *(With particular attention.)* Indeed! Are you ferious?

Amelia. Oh yes!

Baron. Ha! ha! ha!—well we fhall fee!

Amelia. *(Looking up more cheerfully.)* Are you really ferious, dear Father?

Baron. Oh no!

Amelia. *(Dejectedly again.)* No?

Baron. No, Amelia—that will not do—to play fuch a pretty romance, like Abelard and Heloife, or St. Preux and Julie—does not accord with our rank, and the Paftor himfelf is too honourable to think of fuch a thing.

Amelia. You are his benefactor.

Baron. At leaft he thinks me fo.

Amelia. And can any thing be more honourable than to make the daughter of his benefactor happy?

Baron. But if this daughter be a child, and has childifh fancies, and wifhes to day to poffefs a toy, which perhaps to-morrow fhe may throw away in fpleen?

Amelia. Oh no, I am not fuch a child!

Baron.

Baron. Liſten to me, Amelia!—A hundred Fathers would ſay to you, you are of rank yourſelf, you muſt marry a man of rank.—But I do not ſay ſo—my child ſhall not be ſacrificed to prejudice—a woman never can obtain rank by merit, therefore never has reaſon to be proud of it.

Amelia. And therefore—

Baron. Therefore I ſay, in God's name, marry the Paſtor, if you do not find among our young men of rank, one, who for perſon and endowments of heart and mind, correſponds with your ideas.—There may, however, be many of this deſcription—many, perhaps—but as yet you know too little of men in general, to have formed your judgment upon this point. Wait till the enſuing winter—we will ſpend it in town—we will frequent balls and aſſemblies, perhaps you may then think differently.

Amelia. Oh no!—I muſt firſt know a man well, and may even then be deceived in him. But with our Paſtor I have been ſo long, ſo intimately acquainted, that I can read his heart as plainly as my catechiſm.

Baron. Amelia, you have never loved. The Paſtor educated you, and you, ignorant of what love really is, miſtake your ardent gratitude for love.

Amelia. You explained the ſubject to me this morning.

Baron. Did I ſo?—Well, and my queſtions?----

Amelia. All applied to the Paſtor, as if you had penetrated the inmoſt receſſes of my heart.

Baron. Really!—Humph!—Humph!

Amelia. Yes, dear Father, I love, and am alſo beloved.

Baron. Are alſo beloved!—Has he told you ſo?

Amelia. Yes.

Baron. Fye! fye!—that was not right in him.

Amelia. Oh if you knew how I took him by ſurpriſe?

Baron. You took him by ſurpriſe?

Amelia. He came, by your deſire, to ſpeak to me in behalf of the Count,—and I told him I never would marry the Count.

Baron. But would marry him?

Amelia. Yes, him.

Baron. Very frank, by my ſoul?—and what anſwered he?

Amelia. He talked to me about my rank, my family, my uncles and aunts—of his duty to you—and, in ſhort, would

would have perſuaded me to think no more of this. But my heart could not ſuffer itſelf to be perſuaded.

Baron. That was honourable in him—And he will not ſpeak to me on this ſubject?

Amelia. No, he ſaid that was impoſſible!

Baron. So much the better—then I may be ſuppoſed ignorant of the whole affair.

Amelia. But I aſſured him—that I would ſpeak myſelf.

Baron. So much the worſe—that embarraſſes me exceedingly.

Amelia. And now I have done as I ſaid I would.

Baron. Truly you have.

Amelia. Dear Father!

Baron. Dear Child!

Amelia. See the tears will come into my eyes.

Baron. (*Turning from her.*) Repreſs them! (*Both pauſe; Amelia riſes from her ſeat, and bends downwards, as if looking for ſomething.*) What do you look for?

Amelia. I have loſt my needle.

Baron. (*Puſhes back his ſeat and bends forwards to aſſiſt her.*) It cannot be gone ſo far.

Amelia. (*Approaches and falls tenderly on his neck.*) My dear Father!

Baron. Well, and what now?

Amelia. This one requeſt!—

Baron. Let me go!—You make my cheeks wet with your tears!

Amelia. I never can love any other—never can be happy with any other.

Baron. Buffoonery, Amelia!—Childiſhneſs!—be a good girl! (*he ſtroaks her cheeks.*) Sit down again!—we will talk more of this another time—it is not a matter that needs ſuch great haſte—there is no occaſion for an extra-poſt upon the ſubject. The knot that binds you together is tied in a moment—the ſtate of wedlock endures for years. Many a girl ſheds one tear, becauſe ſhe thinks ſhe cannot have her lover, and if ſhe attain him at laſt, perhaps, ſheds tears in torrents that ſhe can never be releaſed from him. Thou haſt relieved thy heart of its oppreſſive burden, and thy Father now bears it in his—bears it for thee, for his dear Amelia.—So ſmall a wound time will ſoon heal, or if it do not, then thou may'ſt chuſe thy phyſician.

Amelia.

Amelia. My dear, kind Father!

Baron. Aye truly, had thy Mother been alive, thou wouldeſt not have eſcaped ſo eaſily—ſhe would have clung to the ſixteen noble generations, which ſhe numbered as her anceſtors.

SCENE VII. *Enter the* PASTOR.

Baron. You are come opportunely.

Paſtor. In conſequence of your order, my Lord, I have releaſed the young man from his priſon He is in the anti-chamber, and wiſhes to return you his thanks in perſon.

Baron. I am pleaſed to hear it—I muſt not ſuffer him to depart empty-handed, I would not confer benefits by halves.

Paſtor. He intreats a few words with you in private.

Baron. In private—Wherefore?

Paſtor. He pleaded his confuſion in the preſence of witneſſes. Perhaps he has ſome diſcovery to make, of which he wiſhes to relieve his heart.

Baron. Well, be it ſo!—Retire Amelia, remain in the anti-chamber with the Paſtor. I wiſh afterwards for ſome converſation with you both. (*Amelia withdraws—the Paſtor opens the door, introduces Frederick, and retires.*)

SCENE VIII. BARON *and* FREDERICK.

Baron. (*Approaching Frederick.*) Depart with God's bleſſing, my friend, you are free. I have ſent to your mother, ſhe is better, for her ſake I pardon you, but beware of a repetition of your offence; highway-robbing is a bad trade. There is a Louis-d'or—ſeek ſome creditable employment, and if I hear that you are diligent and orderly in your behaviour, my doors and my purſe ſhall always be open to aſſiſt you. Go, my friend, and heaven ſupport you!

Fred. (*Taking the Louis-d'or.*) You are a liberal man, free in parting with your money—not ſparing of your good advice. But I have a ſtill greater favour to entreat of you.—You are a rich man, a man of influence, aſſiſt me to obtain juſtice againſt an unnatural Father!

Baron. How!—who is your Father?

Fred. (*With anguiſh.*) A man of rank, lord of much land, and over many tenants—eſteemed at court—honoured

noured in the ſtate—beloved by his peaſants—benevolent, noble-hearted, generous—

Baron. And yet ſuffers his Son to want?

Fred. Yet ſuffers his Son to want!

Baron. Doubtleſs not without reaſon. You were perhaps a wild young fellow, libertine in your principles and practices, gamed, kept a miſtreſs, and your Father therefore thought that following the drum for a few years might have a good effect in correcting ſuch irregularities. And if this be really the caſe, I cannot think your Father has done wrong.

Fred. You miſtake, Sir, my Father knows me not—never has ſeen me—he caſt me off even before my birth.

Baron. How!

Fred. The tears of my Mother are all the inheritance I ever received from my Father. Never has he enquired after me, never concerned himſelf whether I had exiſtence.

Baron. That is bad! (*much confuſed*) very bad indeed!

Fred. I am the unhappy offspring of a ſtolen amour. My poor ſeduced Mother has educated me amidſt ſighs and anguiſh—with the labour of her hands ſhe gained a ſufficiency to enable her, in ſome degree, to cultivate my heart and mind—and I think I am, through her care, become a man, who might be a ſource of joy to any father. But mine, willingly foregoes this pleaſure, and his conſcience leaves him at eaſe reſpecting the fate of his unhappy child.

Baron. At eaſe!—Oh if his conſcience can be at eaſe under ſuch circumſtances, he muſt be a hardened villain indeed!

Fred. As I grew up, and wiſhed no longer to be a burthen upon my indigent mother, I had no reſource but to aſſume theſe garments, and I entered into the ſervice of a volunteer corps—for one illegally born cannot be received as an apprentice by any tradeſman or artiſt.

Baron. Unfortunate young man!

Fred. Thus, amidſt turmoils, paſſed the early years of my life—To the thoughtleſs youth nature generally gives pleaſure as his companion, and through enjoyment ſtrengthens the mind againſt thoſe cares and ſorrows which are the inevitable lot of the maturer man; but the only joys of my youth were coarſe harſh bread, with pure

water,

water, and ſtripes from the ſerjeant's hand. Yet, what ſignifies that to my Father?—his table is ſplendidly ſet out, and to the laſhes of conſcience he is inſenſible.

Baron. (*Aſide*) This young man wrings my heart!

Fred. After a ſeparation of five years from my Mother, I this day returned home, full of love for the country which contained that dear parent—full of the ſweeteſt dreams—of the moſt pleaſing pictures imagination could form. I found my poor mother ſick—reduced to beggary—not having eaten for two days—no bundle of ſtraw on which to lay her head—no ſhelter againſt rain or ſtorms—no compaſſionate heart to cloſe her eyes—no ſpot whereon to die in peace. But what does that concern my father? He has a fine caſtle, ſleeps on ſoft beds of down, and when he dies, the miniſter of religion will in a pompous funeral ſermon, hand down to poſterity his many chriſtian virtues.

Baron. (*ſhuddering.*) Young man, what is thy father's name?

Fred. That he abuſed the weakneſs of a guiltleſs maiden,—deceived her through falſe oaths—that he gave exiſtence to an unhappy wretch, who muſt curſe him for the fatal gift—that he has driven his only ſon almoſt to parricide—Oh theſe are trifles—and when the day of reckoning comes, may all be paid for by a piece of gold?—(*throws the Louis-d'or at the Baron's feet.*)

Baron. (*Half diſtracted.*) Young man, tell me thy father's name!

Fred. Baron Wildenhain! (*The Baron ſtrikes his forehead with both hands, and remains fixed to the ſpot where he ſtands. Frederick proceeds with violent emotion.*) Yes, in this houſe, in this very room, perhaps, was my mother beguiled of her virtue, and I was begotten for the ſword of the executioner. And now, my Lord, I am not free—I am your priſoner—I will not be free.—I am a highway-robber—loudly do I accuſe myſelf as ſuch—you ſhall conſign me over to the hand of juſtice—ſhall conduct me to the place of execution—you ſhall hear how the prieſt ſeeks in vain to calm my mind—ſhall hear how in deſpair I curſe my father—ſhall ſtand by me as the head falls from the trunk—and my blood—your own blood—ſhall ſprinkle your garments.

Baron. Oh hold! hold!

Fred. And when you turn from this ſcene, and deſcend

from

from the ſcaffold—there at its foot ſhall you find my mother, even at the moment that ſhe draws her laſt breath—ſighs out her ſoul in anguiſh!

Baron. Inhuman! hold!

[*The* PASTOR *ruſhes in haſtily.*]

Paſtor. Heaven's what is the matter?—I hear impaſſioned words!—what has been paſſing here?—young man, I hope you have not attempted—

Fred. Yes, ſir, I have attempted to take your office from your hands—I have made a ſinner tremble! (*pointing to the Baron.*) See there—thus after a lapſe of one and twenty years, the injuries ariſing from inordinate paſſions, are avenged.—I am a murderer—I am a highway-robber—but what I feel in this moment is tranſport, is bliſs, compared with the thorns which lacerate his breaſt. I go to ſurrender myſelf up to juſtice, and then at the throne of heaven will I appear a bloody witneſs againſt this man. [*Exit.*

SCENE IX.—*The* BARON—*the* PASTOR.

Paſtor. For heaven's ſake what is the matter?—I cannot underſtand.—

Baron. Oh he is my ſon! he is my ſon!—away, my friend, adviſe me—aſſiſt me, haſten to the poor ſick woman in the village—Frank will ſhew you the way—haſten!—oh haſten!—

Paſtor. But what am I to do?

Baron. Oh God!—your own heart muſt inſtruct you! (*Exit the Paſtor—the* BARON *proceeds with great emotion holding his head with both his hands.*) Am I in my ſenſes?—or are theſe only viſions of fancy?—I have a ſon, a brave, a noble youth, and I have not yet claſped him in my arms, have not preſſed him to my heart—(*calls*) Rodolph! (*Enter a Huntſman.*) Where is he?

Huntſman. Who, my Lord?—the highway-robber?

Baron. Sluggard!—the young man who even now went hence!

Huntſman. He is going before the juſtice—we have ſent after the conſtable.

Baron. Let the conſtable be kicked down ſtairs when he comes—let no one dare to lay hands upon the young man.

Huntſman. (*ſurpriſed.*) Very well, my Lord. (*going.*)

Baron. Stay, Rodolph!

Huntſman. Moſt noble Lord!

Baron. Conduct the young soldier into the green-room by the dining-hall, and attend upon him as his servant.

Huntsman. The count von der Mulde lodges there, my Lord.

Baron. Let him be kicked out, and sent to the devil.— (*The Huntsman stands perplexed, not knowing what he should do, the Baron walks eagerly backwards and forwards.*) I want no son-in-law!—I have a son—a son who shall continue my name, and inherit my estates—a son in whose arms I will die.——Yes, I will atone to him for all—I will suffer no false shame to restrain me!—All my tenants, all my servants, shall know it;—know that I could forget my child—but that I am not hardened in my guilt. Rodolph!

Huntsman. My Lord!

Baron. Conduct him hither!—entreat him to come in, and let all who are in the anti-chamber come with him. (*Rodolph goes out.*) Oh, my heart!—What is it thus makes my blood rush through my veins, that from the crown of my head even to the sole of my foot, I am pulsation all over!—'Tis joy!—joy!—joy!---joy wholly unmerited by me. (*Frederick enters, surrounded by a number of servants, the Baron rushes towards him.*) He comes!——Oh let me clasp thee to this heart! (*He throws himself upon Frederick's neck, and clasps him in his arms.*) My son!!!

END OF ACT IV.

ACT V.

SCENE I. *The Cottager's room, as in the second Act.*
WILHELMINA, *the* COTTAGER, *and his* WIFE.

WILHELMINA.

GOOD Father, go out once more, and fee whether he be not coming.

Cottager. That will not bring him, good woman!——I am but this moment come in, and have looked about every where, and can fee nobody.

Wife. Only have a little patience—who knows whither he may be gone.

Cottager. Yes, indeed, he may be ftraggled into the town.

Wife. True, hufband!—but he won't get much by that; people are hard-hearted enough in the town.

Wilhel. Yet go once more, I entreat you, father!——Perhaps he may foon come now.

Cottager. Directly!—to oblige you! [*Exit.*

Wife. If your fon did but know what God has been pleafed to fend in his abfence, he'd have been here long ago.

Wilhel. I am fo anxious.

Wife. How!—anxious!—One who has fuch a purfe full of money cannot be anxious in mind;—that is to fay, if fhe come by it honeftly.

Wilhel. Where can he ftay fo long?—He has been gone already four hours.——Some misfortune muft have happened to him.

Wife. No, no!—What misfortune fhould happen?—It is ftill broad day-light. Be cheery, and take heart; we'll have a good fupper at night.——Oh, you may live a long time upon that money, and do whatever you pleafe.—Is it not true that our Baron is a fine noble gentleman.

Wilhel. How can he have learnt that I was here?

Wife. Nay, that heaven only knows!——Mr. Frank was fo fecret.

Wilhel. (*Half afide.*) Does he then know me?——It muft be fo, elfe he would not have been fo very liberal.

Wife.

Wife. I do'nt think that follows!—Our good Baron is kind both to thoſe he knows, and to ſtrangers.

(*The Cottager re-enters, ſcratching his head.*)

Wilhel. (*as ſoon as ſhe ſees him*) Well! ſtill no tidings?

Cottager. One might gape till one was blind, and not ſee him at laſt.

Wilhel. Ah, God!—what can come of this!

Cottager. I ſaw our good Paſtor coming round the corner there.

Wilhel. Coming hither?

Cottager. Who knows?——he commonly comes once in three or four weeks, to enquire after us.

Wife. Yes, he is very attentive in viſiting all his pariſhioners, and then he aſks how we go on with our employments, and how we live among each other.---If there's any quarrels or diſcontents among us, he makes them up; ——if any poor man is in great want he aſſiſts him.——You know, huſband, how lately he ſent one of his cows to the lame Michael.

Cottager. Yes, he ſent him the beſt milch-cow, out of his yard.——God bleſs him for it!

Wife. God bleſs him!

SCENE II. *Enter the* PASTOR.

Paſtor. God bleſs you, my children!

Cottager and Wife. Thank you kindly, Sir!

Cottager. You are kindly welcome to us indeed.

Wife. (*reaches a chair, which ſhe wipes with her apron*) Pray ſit down!

Cottager. The weather is warm, let me fetch you a glaſs of beer.

Wife. Or ſome nice juicy pears.

Paſtor. I thank you, good people, but I am not thirſty. You appear to have a viſitor.

Cottager. Ah! dear Sir, ſhe is a poor woman, very ſick and weak—we took her in here from the road.

Paſtor. God will reward your goodneſs.

Cottager. He has rewarded it already.—We are as happy and joyful to day, as if we were going to the wake to-morrow—an't we Bet? (*holds out his hand to his wife.*)

Wife. Yes huſband! (*ſhe takes his hand and ſhakes it heartily.*)

Paſtor. (*to Wilhelmina.*) Who are you, good woman?

Wilhel.

Wilhel. I!—Ah, Sir!—(*in a half whisper*) Oh that we were alone!

Pastor (*to the Cottager*) Be so kind, John, as to leave me alone with this woman for a few minutes—I wish for some private conversation with her.

Cottager. Do you hear, Bet! come along. [*Exeunt.*

SCENE III. *The* PASTOR *and* WILHELMINA.

Pastor. Well, my good woman, we are alone.

Wilhel. Before I tell you what I was, and who I am, allow me to ask you some questions. Are you a native of this country?

Pastor. No, I came from Franconia.

Wilhel. Did you know the worthy old Pastor, your predecessor?

Pastor. No.

Wilhel. (*inquisitively*) You really then do not know any particulars of my unhappy story, and it was merely chance that brought you hither?

Pastor. If you are, indeed, the person I suppose you, and whom I have so long sought, your story is not wholly unknown to me.

Wilhel. Whom you suppose?—and whom you have so long sought?—who then gave you such a commission?

Pastor. A man who interests himself deeply in your fate.

Wilhel. Indeed—Oh quickly tell me then—whom do you suppose me to be?

Pastor. Wilhelmina Böettcher.

Wilhel. Yes, I am the unfortunate, seduced Wilhelmina!—and the man who takes so deep an interest in my fate—I suppose is Baron Wildenhain—he who robbed me of my innocence—the murderer of my father—who for twenty years has consigned me and his child to misery, and who now hopes to atone for all, by a despicable purse of gold. (*Draws out the purse sent her by the Baron.*) I know not with what view you may now come hither, whether to reproach, or to console me, or whether to banish me from these borders, that my presence may not be a reproach to the voluptuary—but one request I have earnestly to make you!—carry back this purse to the man who has ruined me—tell him, that my virtue was not to be be bartered for gold—that gold cannot repay me for my loſt peace of mind, nor can the curſe of an aged parent be redeemed by gold. Tell him, that the poor ſtarving Wilhelmina, though clothed in beggar's rags, is ſtill too proud in ſpirit to receive benefits from her ſeducer. We have no feelings now in common with each other—he deſpiſed my heart—with equal contempt I ſpurn his gold!—he has trampled me under foot—I trample under foot his gold. (*She throws the purſe diſdainfully upon the ground.*) But he ſhall be left to his repoſe—wholly to his repoſe---he ſhall live as hitherto, in mirth and cheerfulneſs, nor ſhall the ſight of Wilhelmina imbitter his pleaſures. As ſoon as I have ſomewhat recovered my ſtrength, I will for ever leave the place, where the name of Wildenhain, and the grave of my poor father, bow me to the ground; and tell him that I knew not he was returned from Franconia, knew not that he was ſo near me!---Aſſure him earneſtly of this, or he may believe that I came hither in ſearch of him.---Oh he muſt not believe that!---And now, Sir, you ſee that your preſence, the object of your viſit, have exhauſted my little ſtrength.---I know not how to ſay more---I know not what more he who ſent you can require of me, (*with indignation.*) Yet one thing farther—perhaps the Baron has recollected, that he once promiſed me marriage---that on his knees before me, he called on God to witneſs his vows, and pledged his honour for their performance---but tell him not to be uneaſy on that account, for the remembrance has long ſince been baniſhed from my boſom.

Paſtor. I have liſtened to you with patient attention, that I might learn your whole ſentiments of the Baron, and your own peculiar ways of thinking. In this unprepared moment, when your full heart overflowed, you doubtleſs have not diſſembled, and I rejoice to find you a woman of the nobleſt ſentiments, worthy of the higheſt atonement that a man of honour---a man of ſtrict honour can make you.---With what ſatisfaction therefore, can I correct an error, which, has perhaps, occaſioned much of the bitterneſs you have expreſſed againſt the Baron. Had he known that the ſick woman in this cottage was Wilhelmina Böettcher, and had ſent to *her* this purſe, he had deſerved that his own ſon ſhould be his murderer!---but no! believe me, no!---this has he not done. Look me in the face, my profeſſion demands con-

fidence,

fidence, but, independently of that, you ſurely would believe me incapable of a falſhood—and I moſt ſolemnly aſſure you, that it was chance alone, made you the object of his bounty, which he believed was exerciſed towards an entire ſtranger.

Wilhel. How, Sir!---Would you perſuade me, that ſuch a preſent as this was the effect of chance?---To a ſtranger one ſends a florin, a dollar, but not a purſe of gold.

Paſtor. I grant it is extraordinary---but the occaſion was extraordinary. Your ſon—

Wilhel. What! my Son?

Paſtor. Be calm. An affectionate Son begged for his Mother---that affected the Baron.

Wilhel. Begged of the Baron!---of his Father!

Paſtor. Even ſo!—but underſtand, that neither knew the other—and that the mother received this preſent for the ſake of the ſon.

Wilhel. Knew not each other!—And where is my ſon?

Paſtor. At the caſtle.

Wilhel. And ſtill are they unknown to each other?

Paſtor. No—all is now revealed, and I am ſent hither by the Baron, not to an unknown ſick-woman, but to Wilhelmina Böettcher, not with money, but with a commiſſion to act as my own heart ſhall dictate.

Wilhel. Your heart!—oh, Sir, pledge not your feelings for thoſe of this obdurate man!—Yet will the woman forget, what ſhe has ſuffered for his ſake, if he only will atone for it to the mother—the woman will pardon him, if he deſerve the Mother's thanks. In what ſtate then is my Frederick—how has the baron received him?

Paſtor. I left him overcome by violent emotions—it was even then the moment of diſcovery—nothing was yet decided—yet; doubtleſs, at this inſtant the ſon is claſped in his father's arms. I will warrant that his heart—

Wilhel. Again his heart!—heaven's how is the heart of this man thus ſuddenly changed?—for twenty years deaf to the voice of nature—

Paſtor. You do him injuſtice!—hear before you judge him. Many errors appear to us at the firſt view deteſtable—when if we knew all that led to them, all the intervening

vening circumſtances which inſenſibly prompted to the deed, all the trifles whoſe iufluence is ſo imperceptible, and yet ſo great, how might our opinions be altered.—Could we have accompanied the offender ſtep by ſtep, inſtead of, as now, ſeeing only the firſt, the tenth, and the twentieth, often indeed, ſhould we exculpate, where we at preſent condemn. Far be it from me to defend the Baron's miſconduct, but this I dare aſſert, that even a good man may once in his life be guilty of a lapſe, without deſerving to forfeit entirely his character for goodneſs. Where is the demi-god, who can dare to vaunt, that his conſcience is clear, pure as falling ſnow!—and if ſuch a boaſter live, for God's-ſake truſt him not, he is far more dangerous than a repentant ſinner.—Pardon my diffuſeneſs—in a few words you ſhall now have the Baron's ſtory ſince your ſeparation.—At that time he loved you moſt ſincerely, but the fear of his rigid mother prevented the fulfilment of his vows. The war recalled him to the field, where he was ſeverely wounded, made a priſoner, and for a whole year was confined to his bed, unable to write to you, or to obtain any information concerning you—Then did your image firſt begin to grow fainter in his mind. In conſequence of his dangerous wounds, he was carried from the field of battle to a neighbouring manſion, the owner of which was a man of rank and benevolence, poſſeſſed of a large eſtate, and the father of a beautiful daughter. The maiden was particularly pleaſed with the young man, ſcarcely ever left his bed-ſide, nurſed him like a ſiſter, and ſhed tears for his ſufferings, to which the Baron's heart could not be inſenſible. Philanthropy and gratitude knit the bands, which death tore aſunder but a few weeks ſince. Thus was the remembrance of you entirely obliterated. He exchanged his native country for a noble reſidence in Franconia; he became a huſband, a father, and employed himſelf in the improvement of his eſtates—no object that he beheld reminded him of you, nor could any thing revive your image in his heart, till his life became imbittered by domeſtic feuds. Too late he diſcovered in his wife a proud, imperious woman, a ſpoiled child poſſeſſing a ſpirit of contradiction, and pertinaciouſly adhering to her own opinions. She ſeemed to have reſcued him from death, merely to torment him to

death

death herſelf. Chance at that time conducted me to his houſe—I gained his friendſhip—I became the inſtructor of his only daughter, and was ſoon admitted to his confidence.—Oh how often has he with anguiſh of heart, ſaid, " This woman revenges on me the wrongs of my Wilhelmina."—How often has he curſed the wealth which his wife brought him, and in fancy enjoyed a leſs brilliant, but more happy lot, in your arms. When at length this living became vacant, and he offered me the cure, the firſt words with which he accompanied the propoſal were, " my Friend, there will you learn what is become of my Wilhelmina."—Every letter that I afterwards received from him, contained this exclamation —" Still no tidings of my Wilhelmina!"—Theſe letters are now in my poſſeſſion—you may ſee them. I never was able to diſcover the place of your abode—fate prevented it—having in its view this more important day.

Wilhel. You have affected me much—and the emotions which I feel preſs conviction to my heart. How will all this end?—What now is to become of me?

Paſtor. The Baron did not indeed ſignify to me his intentions ſhould you be found, but your wrongs demand atonement, and I know but of one way in which it can be made.—Exalted woman! If your ſtrength will permit you to accompany me—my carriage waits—the road is ſhort and eaſy.

Wilhel. I go with you?—Go before the Baron in theſe rags?

Paſtor. And wherefore not?

Wilhel. Will they not reproach him?

Paſtor. Noble-minded woman!—come with me then; we will ſtop at my houſe; my ſiſter will quickly furniſh you with clothes.

Wilhel. But ſhall I find my Frederick at the caſtle?

Paſtor. Moſt certainly!

Wilhel. (*riſing.*) Well!—for his ſake I will ſubmit to this arduous taſk!—He is the only branch on which my hopes ſtill bloſſom—the reſt are all withered, dead!—But where are my good Hoſt and Hoſteſs, that I may take my leave, and thank them?

Paſtor. (*takes up the purſe, goes to the door and calls.*) Here, Neighbour!—John!

SCENE IV.

SCENE IV. *Enter* COTTAGER *and his* WIFE.

Cottager. Here I am!

Wife. Thank God, ſhe is upon her legs once more! I am heartily glad of it.

Paſtor. My good friends, I will take this woman with me—ſhe will have better accommodations.

Cottager. Yes, indeed!—ſhe is but badly off here.

Wife. We were glad to do the beſt we could for her, but we could do but ſorrily after all.

Paſtor. You have acted like worthy people—take that as a reward for your kindneſs! (*Offers the purſe to the Cottager, who puts his hands before him, plays with his fingers in his waiſtcoat, looks at the money, and ſhakes his head.*) Will you not take it? (*Offers it to the wife; ſhe plays with her apron, looks at it with half-averted eyes, and ſhakes her head.*) What is your objection?

Cottager. Pray don't take it amiſs, good Sir; I can't think of being paid for doing my duty.

Wife. (*looking up to heaven*) There we look for our reward.

Paſtor. (*laying a hand on the ſhoulder of each, much affected*) And there you will be rewarded—Heaven bleſs you both!

Wilhel. You will not refuſe my thanks?

Cottager. You are kindly welcome.

Wife. Yes, you are heartily welcome.

Wilhel. Farewell, kind people!—(*She ſhakes them both by the hand.*)

Cottager. Farewell, farewell!—I hope you'll ſoon be better.

Wife. And if you ever come this way, pray call in.

Paſtor. God preſerve you! (*Offers his arm to Wilhelmina, who takes hold of it, wipes the tears from her eyes, and ſupports herſelf by a ſtick in the other hand.*)

Cottager. Adieu, good Paſtor! (*Pulls off his hat, and makes many ſcrapings with his foot.*)

Wife. And I thank you kindly for this viſit.

Both. And we hope you'll come again ſoon. (*They go to the door with the Paſtor and Wilhelmina.*)

Cottager. (*taking his wife by the hand*) Well, Bet, what think you? How ſhall we ſleep to-night?

Wife. (*preſſing his hand*) As ſound as tops. [*Exeunt.*

SCENE V. *A Room in the Castle.*

The BARON *sits on a sopha, exhausted by various emotions:* FREDERICK *stands by, bending over him, and pressing one of the Baron's hands between his.*

Baron. So, you have really seen service—smelt gunpowder—I'd lay my life, young man, that as Frederick von Wildenhain, you had been spoiled both by father and mother; but as Frederick Böettcher, you are grown to be a brave fellow. Thou hast hitherto been exposed to hardships and dangers—thy youthful path has not been strewed with roses!—Well, well, Frederick, it shall be otherwise now—the future shall reward thee for the past. The opprobium of thy birth shall be removed---Indeed it shall. I will publicly acknowledge thee as my only son, and as heir to my estates!—What say'st thou to this?

Fred. And my mother?

Baron. Oh, fear not that she shall starve!——Thou can'st not suppose thy father will do things by halves. Knowest thou not that Wildenhain is one of the best estates in this country, and only a mile from hence lies Wellendorf, also a little estate of mine? Besides, through my wife, God rest her soul! I have three large manors in Franconia.

Fred. But my mother?

Baron. I was going to say, that your mother shall have her choice of an abode. If she does not like Franconia, she may remain at Wellendorf. There is a neat house, neither too large nor too small—a pretty garden, and in a delightful country—in short, a paradise in miniature. There shall she want for nothing—there shall a happy old age smooth the furrows which a youth of sorrow has made in her cheeks.

Fred. (*starting back*) How!

Baron. Yes, indeed!—And you know, Frederick, as the distance is not great, in the morning, should we be inclined to make your mother a visit, 'tis only to saddle the horses, and we can be there in an hour.

Fred. Indeed!—And by what name shall my mother be called?

Baron. (*confused*) How?

Fred. Is she to be considered as your housekeeper, or your mistress?

Baron.

Baron. Fool!

Fred. I underſtand you!—and will withdraw myſelf, my father, that you may have time to conſider of your reſolution; only I aſſure you, by all that is moſt dear, moſt ſacred to me, (nor can any thing ſhake my determination) that my fate is inſeparably united to my mother's—it muſt be Wilhelmina von Wildenhain, and Frederick von Wildenhain, or Wilhelmina Böettcher and Frederick Böettcher. [*Exit.*

Baron. So!—What would he then?—Surely he does not mean that I ſhould marry his mother?—Young man! young man! thou muſt not preſume to preſcribe laws to thy father!—I thought I had arranged every thing admirably well—I was as happy as a king—I had relieved my conſcience of a burden, and was recovering my breath, then comes this fellow and rolls another great ſtone in the path over which I muſt ſtumble. Well, well, friend Conſcience, God be thanked, thou and I are friends again.—Hey! how's this? What am I to underſtand?—Thou art ſilent—or rather ſeemeſt to murmur a little!

SCENE VI. *Enter the* PASTOR.

Baron. You are come in happy time, my friend; my conſcience and I have commenced a ſuit, and ſuch ſuits properly belong to your juriſdiction.

Paſtor. Your conſcience is in the right.

Baron. Hey, hey, Mr. Judge, not ſo partial if you pleaſe!---you know not yet what the queſtion is.

Paſtor. Conſcience is always in the right, for it never ſpeaks but when it is in the right.

Baron. Well,---but I am not yet certain whether it ſpeaks, or is ſilent, only in ſuch caſes perſons of your profeſſion have quicker ears than our own. Liſten then, a few words will ſtate the caſe.---I have found my ſon, (*Clapping his hand on his ſhoulder*) a fine, noble youth, good Paſtor! full of fire as a Frenchman, proud as an Engliſhman, and full of honour as a German.——Be this as it may, I mean to remove the opprobrium of his illegitimacy.---Am I not right in this?

Paſtor. Perfectly right!

Baron. And his mother ſhall, in her old age, lead an affluent and happy life. I will give her my eſtate of Wellendorf, there may ſhe live, form it according to her taſte, grow young again in her ſon, revive in her grand-children.---Am I not right in this?

Paſtor. No.

Baron. (*Starting back.*) No!---What then ſhould I do?

Paſtor. Marry her!

Baron. How!—Marry her?

Paſtor. Baron Wildenhain is a man who never acts without ſufficient reaſon.---I ſtand here as the advocate of your conſcience, and requeſt to know upon what grounds you now proceed---Then ſhall you hear what I have to ſay.

Baron. Would you have me marry a beggar?

Paſtor. (*after a pauſe*) Is that all?

Baron. (*confuſed*) No,---I have further grounds:---much further!

Paſtor. May I requeſt to know them?

Baron. (*ſtill much confuſed*) I am a Nobleman.

Paſtor. What more?

Baron. People will point their fingers at me.

Paſtor. Proceed.———

Baron. My relations will look aſkance at me.

Paſtor. Well.——

Baron. And---and---(*very haſtily*) plague take it, I can recollect nothing more!

Paſtor. Now, then, it is my turn to ſpeak. But before I begin, let me put a few queſtions to you: Did Wilhelmina, through levity or coquetry, lay herſelf open to ſeduction.

Baron. No, no, ſhe was always a modeſt, prudent girl.

Paſtor. Did it coſt you much trouble to ſubdue her virtue.

Baron. (*ſhortly*) Yes.

Paſtor. Did you not promiſe her marriage? (*the Baron heſitates, the Paſtor aſks again more earneſtly*) Did you not promiſe her marriage?

Baron. Yes!

Paſtor. And called God to witneſs your promiſe?

Baron. Yes!

Paſtor. And pledged your honour for its performance?

Baron. (*impatiently*) The devil!---Yes!

Paſtor. Well then, my Lord,---God was your witneſs—God, who ſaw you at that moment, and who ſees you now.—Your honour was your pledge, which you muſt redeem, if you are indeed a man of honour. I now ſtand before you, impreſſed with the dignity of my ſublime vocation, and dare ſpeak to you as to the loweſt of your peaſants;

my

my duty requires it, and I will fulfil my duty, even at the hazard of your friendſhip. Did you, as a thoughtleſs youth, who lives only for the preſent moment, ſeduce an innocent girl without thinking on the conſequences; but, in maturer years, repenting of your youthful follies, have you to the utmoſt of your power repaired your faults, then are you indeed a man deſerving the eſteem of the honeſt and the virtuous.---But---has the voluptuous youth, through wicked ſnares, involved a guiltleſs creature in miſery, and deprived a maiden of her virtue, her happineſs, to ſatisfy the paſſion of a moment? did he pledge his word of honour in intoxication, and offer up his conſcience as a ſacrifice to his deſires, and believes he that all is to be atoned by a handful of gold, of which chance alone makes him the poſſeſſor.---Oh, does not ſuch an one deſerve——Pardon my warmth, my lord! it might injure a good cauſe, were it not here moſt natural.—Farewell the good old days of chivalry. The virtues of our anceſtors, their high ſenſe of honour, their reverence for female delicacy, are buried in one common grave; nothing now remains but the moſt trivial or the worſt part, of thoſe times, their titles, and their ſingle combats. A victory over innocence is, in theſe days, conſidered as a deed of heroiſm, of which the conqueror vaunts over his bottle, while the poor object of ſeduction, drowned in her tears, curſes the deſtroyer of her honour and peace of mind, and perhaps harbours the horrid thought of being herſelf the murderer of the infant ſhe bears. I repeat, then, my Lord, that you ought to keep your word, even though you were a prince! A prince may indeed be releaſed by the ſtate from its performance, but never can be acquitted by his own conſcience!---Have you not reaſon then to thank God, that you are not a prince? that it is in your power to purchaſe repoſe of heart, that higheſt of all treaſures, at ſo cheap a price? --The reſolution to marry Wilhelmina is not even a merit, for this union will increaſe your own happineſs. 'Tis pity indeed that it coſts you no ſacrifice, that your whole fortune is not at ſtake; then might you well come forth, and ſay, do I not act nobly? I marry Wilhelmina!---But now, ſince Wilhelmina brings you ſuch a dowry, greater than any princeſs could beſtow---repoſe to your conſcience, and a ſon ſo worthy of your affection.---Now may you well exclaim---Wiſh me joy, my friend! I marry Wilhelmina!

Baron.

Baron. (*During this ſpeech he has appeared extremely agitated, now walking backwards and forwards, then pauſing—one moment teſtifying indignation, the next the moſt affecting emotions—at length when the Paſtor has done ſpeaking, he approaches him with open arms, preſſes him to his boſom, and exclaims*) My Friend! wiſh me joy, I marry Wilhelmina!!!

Paſtor. (*returning his embrace.*) I moſt ſincerely wiſh you joy!

Baron. Where is ſhe?—have you ſeen her?

Paſtor. She is in your ſtudy. To avoid obſervation I conducted her in through the garden.

Baron. Well then, this ſhall be the wedding day!—You, my Friend, ſhall give us your bleſſing this very evening.

Paſtor. Oh no! not ſo haſtily—not ſo privately. The whole village was witneſs to Wilhelmina's ſhame—it muſt alſo be witneſs to the reſtoration of her honour. Three Sundays ſucceſſively muſt the banns be publiſhed; are you content that it ſhall be ſo?

Baron. I am content.

Paſtor. And then will we ſolemnize a happy nuptial feaſt, and the whole village ſhall unite in jubilee on the occaſion. Are you ſatisfied?

Baron. Perfectly!

Paſtor. Is the ſuit now decided?—is your conſcience eaſy?

Baron. Completely ſo—I wiſh only that the firſt interview were over. I feel the ſame ſhame in appearing before her whom I have injured, as a thief before the man he has robbed.

Paſtor. Be calm!—Wilhelmina's heart is your judge.

Baron. And then—Wherefore ſhould I not confeſs it? prejudices are like old Wounds! when the weather changes they ſtill ſmart.—I—I cannot help feeling ſomewhat aſhamed when I think that all muſt be known to my daughter—to the count—to all my domeſtics. I would it were already over—till it is, I will not ſee Wilhelmina, that when we meet, nothing may remain but joy—but tranſport!—Frank! (*calls to a Huntſman who enters*) Where are my daughter and the count?

Huntſman. In the dining-room, my Lord.

Baron. Deſire them to come hither. [*Exit Huntſman.* Remain here with me, good Paſtor! that the Coxcomb with his privy-chamber airs, may not diſconcert me. I

ſhall

ſhall ſpeak my mind to him clearly and conciſely, and when that is done, let his horſes be put to the carriage, and he may go with his *pommade* to the devil.

SCENE VII. *Enter* AMELIA *and the* COUNT.

Count. Nous voila à vos ordres, mon Colonel! we have taken a moſt *delicieuſe promenade.* Wildenhain is an earthly Paradiſe, and poſſeſſes an Eve, who reſembles the Mother of all mankind—only *il manquoit un Adam* who might take with extaſies from her hand even the Apple of death itſelf!—But now he is found, *cet Adam!*—he is found!

Baron. Who is found?—Frederick, but not Adam!

Count. Frederick!---Who is this Frederick?

Baron. My ſon!---my only Son!

Count. Comment? your Lordſhip's ſon?—*Mon Pere* informed me that you had only this daughter.

Baron. Your *Pere* could not know that I had a ſon, for I knew it myſelf but a few minutes ago.

Count. Vouz parlez des enigmes.

Baron. In ſhort, the young man who attacked us on the highway to day—You may remember it well, as you ran away ſo faſt.

Count. I have a confuſed remembrance of it. But——

Baron. Well, he is my ſon!

Count. He?---how is it poſſible to believe this?

Baron. Yes, he! (*aſide to the Paſtor*) Speak for me, I am aſhamed before that coxcomb.

Paſtor. A man like you abaſhed before ſuch an animal!

Baron. He is my natural ſon.---But what of that---before the expiration of many weeks, I ſhall marry his mother, and whoever ſhall dare to ſneer at it, ſhall be properly chaſtiſed. Yes, yes, Amelia, look up my child, you have, found a brother.

Amelia. (*with extacy*) Are you not joking?---may I believe it?

Count. And may one aſk the name of his Mother?---Is ſhe of Family?

Baron. She is---good Paſtor, tell him what ſhe is!

Paſtor. A beggar.

Count. (*laughing*) *Vouz badinez!*

Paſtor. Her name, if you wiſh to know it, Wilhelmina Böettcher.

Count. Von Böettcher? I never heard of the family.

Baron.

Baron. She belongs to the family of honeſt people, and that is a damn'd ſmall one.

Count. Quite a *Meſalliance* then?

Paſtor. Generoſity and integrity, unite themſelves with love and conſtancy.---Call that a *Meſalliance* if you pleaſe.

Count. It muſt be acknowledged, that one ought to be *un Œdipe*, in order to develope all theſe riddles. *Un fils naturel!---à la bonne heure, mon Colonel!*---Why I have two. There muſt be *moments* in a man's life, when if a pretty girl fall in his way---ſuch things happen every day. But *mon dieu!* one never troubles one's head with ſuch beings---unleſs to put them to ſome trade perhaps, and ſo make them uſeful in the world. Mine are both to be made *friſeurs.*

Baron. And mine ſhall be a nobleman—and inherit the eſtates of Wildenhain and Wellendorf.

Count. Me voila ſtupefait!---Moſt charming young lady, I muſt plead your cauſe—they are *au point de vous ecraſer.*

Amelia. Do not give yourſelf that trouble.

Count. La fille unique!---L'unique heritiere.

Amelia. Il me reſte l'amour de mon pere!

Baron. Bravo, Amelia!---bravo!—Come hither, and let me give you a kiſs! (*Amelia flies into his arms*) Count, you will do me a favour, if you will take yourſelf away. A ſcene may, perhaps, paſs here, from which you will derive no ſatisfaction.

Count. De tout mon cœur!—At preſent, if I miſtake not, we have *clair de lune*, and I ſhall be enabled this very evening to return into the town.

Baron. As you pleaſe.

Count. A dire vrai, mon Colonel! I came not hither to ſeek a *voleur de grand chemin* as my brother-in-law, nor a *Gueuſe* as my ſtep-mother. *Henri! Henri!* [*Skips out.*

SCENE VIII. *The* BARON, AMELIA, *and the* PASTOR.

Baron. (*ſtill claſping Amelia in his arms*) Ah, I breathe more freely!—And now a word with you, my Amelia— Twenty years ago, your father was guilty of a lapſe— ſeduced a poor girl, and gave exiſtence to a child, who till this day has wandered about the world in meanneſs and poverty. The circumſtance has preſſed upon my mind like a rock of granite---You may remember how many an evening I have ſpent in gloom and deep dejection

jection—with my eyes fixed as I ſat in my arm-chair ſmoking my pipe---not hearing you when you ſpoke, not ſmiling when you careſſed me---then was it that my conſcience upbraided me---that all my wealth, my rank, nor even you, my child, could procure me the repoſe which a ſpotleſs mind alone can feel. Now I have found both wife and ſon; and this worthy man, (*pointing to the Paſtor*) as well as this, (*pointing to his heart*) both tell me 'tis my duty publicly to acknowledge them as ſuch. What think you?

Amelia. (*careſſing him.*) My Father need not aſk that.

Baron. Will not the loſs you muſt experience, coſt you one ſigh? Will a father's repoſe pay you for all?

Amelia. What loſs?

Baron. You were conſidered as my only heireſs.

Amelia. (*tenderly reproving him.*) Oh my Father!

Baron. You loſe two fine eſtates.

Amelia. But a Brother's love will amply repay them.

Baron. And mine! (*preſſing her eagerly to his boſom.*)

Paſtor. (*turning aſide.*) Oh why not mine alſo!

Baron. (*to the Paſtor.*) My friend, for a victory over *one* prejudice, I have to thank you!—for a victory over a ſecond, I muſt thank myſelf!---A man like you, the teacher, and the image of virtue, raiſes his profeſſion to one of the nobleſt that the world can boaſt. Were all your brethren like yourſelf, chriſtianity might well be proud of them!---you are a NOBLE MAN---I am only a Nobleman---or, if I am now likely to become more, it is to you I ſhall be indebted for the change. I am indeed very much your debtor---Amelia, will you pay for me? (*Amelia looks at her Father doubtfully for a few moments, then lets fall her hands, turns to the Paſtor, and flies into his arms.*)

Paſtor. (*in the utmoſt aſtoniſhment.*) My God!---my Lord Baron.

Baron. Silence, ſilence! Not a word.

Amelia. (*kiſſing him*) Silence, ſilence! You, indeed, love me! (*The Paſtor looſens himſelf from her arms, burſts into tears, attempts to ſpeak, but is unable—he goes up to the Baron, takes his hand, and is about preſſing it to his mouth, when the Baron withdraws it, and preſſes him in his arms.*)

Amelia. Oh, I am ſo happy!

Baron. (*withdrawing his arms from the Paſtor*)—Enough, enough!—Oh, I could cry like a child!—Suffer me, ſuffer me to compoſe myſelf for a few moments—I have yet another ſcene to come, more heart-affecting than even this.—Now, deareſt Frederick, in a few minutes all ſhall be accompliſhed, and the laſt rays of the declining ſun ſhall beam upon the happieſt group in Nature's wide-extended kingdom.—Where is Wilhelmina?

Paſtor. I will fetch her.

Baron. Stop!—my mind is agitated!—my heart ſo throbs!—one moment to recover myſelf. (*He walks backwards and forwards, breathes with difficulty, and caſts his eyes frequently towards the door of the adjoining room.*) That way will ſhe come—that was my mother's chamber—thence have I often ſeen her come—have feaſted on her ſweet ſmile—how can I bear now to ſee her darkened ſorrow-worn countenance?—Frederick muſt plead for me—Where is my Frederick? (*calls*) Frank! (*Huntſman enters*) Where is my ſon?

Huntſman. In his room.

Baron. Deſire him to come hither! (*to the Paſtor*) Now!—my heart beats eagerly! Haſte! Haſte!—conduct her in! (*The Paſtor goes out at the ſide-door—the Baron turns towards it, but ſtarts back ſome ſteps, while all his features betray the greateſt agitation*).

SCENE IX. *Enter the* PASTOR, *conducting in* WILHELMINA—*the* BARON *catches her ſpeechleſs in his arms—ſhe almoſt faints. The* BARON *and* PASTOR *place her in a chair; the* BARON *kneels before her, with one arm round her waiſt, and her hand preſſed in the other.*

Baron. Wilhelmina! know you not my voice?

Wilhel. (*tenderly and faintly*) Wildenhain!

Baron. Can you forgive me?

Wilhel. I forgive you freely!

Fred. (*enters haſtily*) My mother's voice!—Oh, mother!—father! (*He throws himſelf on his knees by the other ſide of his mother—ſhe bends tenderly over both—the Paſtor ſtands with his eyes gratefully turned towards heaven—Amelia leans on his ſhoulder, and wipes the tears from her eyes*).

The curtain falls.

END OF THE PLAY.

SKETCH
OF THE
LIFE AND WRITINGS
OF
KOTZEBUE;

Extracted principally from a PAPER *in the* MONTHLY MAGAZINE *of August last.*

By Dr. WILLICH, *Physician to the Saxon Embassy.*

KOTZEBUE ftands equally high in the lift of German literati, confidered both as a dramatic writer, and as a writer of novels and romances. In the former line he is juftly allowed to rank among the moft celebrated names which the prefent times can boaft, and not to be inferior in excellence to Schiller, Schröder, Wieland, or Klopftock.

He is a native of Weimar in Saxony, a fmall but highly-polifhed city, which has frequently been called "*Paris in miniature.*" He was educated under the care and tuition of the late profeffor Mufæus * of Weimar, of whom he foon became a favourite pupil, and from whom he imbibed an early attachment to the Mufes. This tafte he farther cultivated by his unremitting attention to the dramatic performances at his native town, which were then in great repute on account of the refined tafte and correct judgment of the actors and audience. KOTZEBUE's decided predilection for the drama, in theory as

* The name of MUSÆUS is never mentioned in Germany but with pleafure and refpect. His "Popular Tales of the Germans" were tranflated into Englifh, about feven or eight years fince; and although the fimplicity and humour of Mufæus's fpirit are not fully transfufed into the tranflation, yet every candid reader muft allow that the work poffeffes uncommon merit, and will confider it as an ample teftimony of the author's talents and ingenuity.

well

well as in practice, is obvious from ſeveral paſſages alluding to this ſubject in his own works: yet it is certain that he never performed on any public ſtage, but that all his attempts as an actor were confined to private theatres eſtabliſhed among ſelect parties of literary friends. Thus he gained the double advantage of at once gratifying his inclinations by indulging himſelf in his favourite amuſement, and at the ſame time of exhibiting his dramatic compoſitions to a contracted circle of candid and diſcerning critics, and thereby obtaining a juſt deciſion on their merits before he ventured to preſent them to the public.

KOTZEBUE was educated for the law, which he practiſed for a ſucceſſion of years in various eminent ſtations, till he was appointed preſident of the high college of juſtice in the Ruſſian province of Livonia. While in this ſituation, he appears, in conjunction with other friends, to have eſtabliſhed a private theatre at Revel, in which ſome of his pieces were firſt performed; that before us being one of the number. The majority of his dramatic works were, indeed, written during the time of his reſidence in Livonia, as well as many of his miſcellaneous compoſitions in the department of the *Belles-Lettres.*

That his writings ſhould be ſo multifarious is the more ſurprizing, as his leiſure time muſt till latterly have been very inconſiderable; ſince, during the period that he held the diſtinguiſhed office above-mentioned, the variety and importance of his other avocations muſt have required nearly the whole of his attention. Fortunately, however, for the Muſes, and particularly thoſe of the German ſtage, he met with a number of invidious opponents in Livonia, who magnified every trifling foible of his private conduct into a crime of the firſt magnitude, and perſecuted him with ſuch unrelenting malignity, that he thought proper to retire from his ſplendid office of ſtate, and devote the remainder of his life to a more grateful public. Hence he betook himſelf entirely to literary purſuits; and, having quitted the Ruſſian dominions, he repaired to the court of Vienna, where he very ſoon obtained the appointment of *Poet-laureat to the Emperor, and Dramatiſt to the Imperial Theatre*; in which ſituation his merits and talents now meet with their juſt reward, in the very high degree of public eſteem in which they are held, and which they ſo amply deſerve.

It

It is unneceſſary here to detail the complicated intrigues carried on under the late Empreſs of Ruſſia in every province of her extenſive empire, and the frequent perſecutions which foreigners promoted to office ſuſtained from the ſemi-barbarous natives. Let it ſuffice to obſerve, that they too often ſucceeded in their nefarious deſigns againſt thoſe aliens whom they hated, both on account of the ſuperiority of their talents, and their abhorrence of Ruſſian ſloth and drunkenneſs. KOTZEBUE was one of the many objects of perſecution in Ruſſia, although his moral character may fairly be concluded to have been unexceptionable, as it is ſcarcely credible that the Emperor of Germany would otherwiſe have conferred upon him ſuch diſtinguiſhed marks of his favour. It is probable that one principal cauſe of his being obliged to leave the Ruſſian dominions, was the diſapprobation he drew upon himſelf on account of his celebrated work, called "*Count Benjowſky, or the Conſpiracy of Kamſchatka,*" which contains many private anecdotes relative to the cruelties practiſed by order of the Czarina towards her oppreſſed and enſlaved ſubjects.

The merits of our author in the wide field of the drama are now much known, and begin to be duly appreciated in this country, through thoſe of his productions which have already been tranſlated into the Engliſh language. It is to be regretted, however, that German tranſlations often appear in a very mutilated and metamorphoſed ſtate before the Engliſh public; ſince, on this account, it is not very eaſy juſtly to aſcertain the due and relative merits of either the author or tranſlator. Of about thirty dramatic pieces, of various merit, publiſhed by KOTZEBUE, four had appeared in an Engliſh dreſs prior to the work now before us: "*Miſanthropy and Repentance*"—"*The Negro Slaves*"—*Count Benjowſky*"—and "*The Indians in England**." The firſt of theſe, under the title of "*The Stranger,*" was performed with great applauſe (though with very great alterations) at Drury-Lane theatre laſt winter, and for a conſiderable part of the ſeaſon attracted brilliant and crouded audi-

* Since the firſt edition of the preſent work was publiſhed, a tranſlation of another of KOTZEBUE's plays, "*Adelaide von Wulfingen,*" by Mr. THOMSON, the tranſlator of "*The Stranger,*" has been advertiſed.

ences. "*The Natural Son,*" under the title of "*Lovers' Vows,*" promifes to be an equally great favourite at Covent-Garden theatre during the enfuing winter.

The fuccefs of thefe pieces holds forth great encouragement to tranflate others of KOTZEBUE's dramatic works, which would doubtlefs prove equally interefting to an Englifh audience. That more of thefe admirable productions have not hitherto been brought forwards to public notice, may be afcribed partly to the great difference which has been fuppofed to fubfift between the national tafte and manners of the Englifh and thofe of the Germans, particularly with regard to their dramatic compofitions; and partly to a certain marked peculiarity in whatever comes from the pen of KOTZEBUE, which characterifes and diftinguifhes his productions from thofe of all other modern writers. But the experiment has been made, and the event has proved this idea to be unfounded.

All KOTZEBUE's writings fpeak a liberal and enlarged mind, full of benevolence and philanthropy. His knowledge of the human heart and its fecret meanders is unqueftionably great: he has not only made the prevailing manners, oddities, and vices of the age, but alfo man himfelf, as influenced by a variety of ardent paffions, the fubject of his minuteft refearch. Few perfons have ever attained to his excellence in delineating whimfical and impaffioned characters; and in fcenes drawn from private and domeftic life, he eminently excels his cotemporary rivals both in the unaffected delicacy of the fentiments he conveys, and the freedom and precifion with which he introduces them. His language, if not remarkably brilliant, is yet generally correct, and dignified; his comic fcenes abound with genuine wit and humour, untinctured with the vulgarity into which writers in that line are too apt to deviate; and his pathetic fcenes are no lefs diftinguifhed for thofe delicate touches of nature which appeal in the moft forcible manner to the heart. His plans are formed with great art, and developed for the moft part in an unexpected, yet probable and fuccefsful manner.

To the morality of the work now before us, as well as to that of "*Mifanthropy and Repentance,*" objections have been made as not prefenting fufficient difcouragement againft a lapfe from virtue in the female fex; fince, in both inftances, the heroines, notwithftanding their paft tranftranſgreſſions, are finally reſtored to their ſtation in ſociety. But this objection does not ſeem well-founded, and to be made rather from taking only a ſuperficial glance over the ſurface of the ſubject, than from diving into its inmoſt receſſes. Surely in neither caſe is the fate of the offender ſo alluring as to offer any attraction to others to follow their ſteps; on the contrary, the ſufferings endured by both in conſequence of their reſpective faults, hold out a forcible warning to beware of the errors which led to ſuch miſery. Neither does their reſtoration at laſt ſeem a violation of that ſtrict juſtice which their offences demanded, ſince to teach the tranſgreſſor that no length of ſuffering, and ſeverity of repentance, can atone for ſuch a lapſe, muſt tend to diſcourage every attempt to reformation, inſtead of exciting to all poſſible endeavours for its attainment. The great cauſe of virtue ſeems beſt ſupported by painting, in forcible colours, the inevitable miſery attendant upon guilt, yet at the ſame time holding out every encouragement that can be offered, to thoſe who have unfortunately ſwerved from their duty, to ſeek by the moſt ſtrenuous efforts to regain the height they have loſt. In this point of view the morality of theſe pieces will appear unexceptionable; or, if any objection is to be made againſt it, it ſhould rather ſeem to be on a different ground. That the ſufferings of WILHELMINA in "*The Natural Son*," are more ſevere and more protracted than thoſe of EULALIA in "*Miſanthropy and Repentance*;" whereas the crime of the latter, as a married woman deſerting her huſband and children for another man, is beyond compariſon greater than that of the former.

Only one of KOTZEBUE's romances, it is believed, has yet appeared in an Engliſh garb, "*Ildegerte Queen of Norway*," tranſlated alſo by Mr. THOMSON. In this the author entirely quits the path of nature, in tracing the meanders of which he is ſo eminently ſucceſsful, and deviates into that of extravagant imagination where he does not appear equally happy. Still this romance, if not poſſeſſing a like degree of intereſt with ſome other of his works, as a memorial of the extent and variety of his talents, is well worthy of notice. His more ſimple tales, however, claim, and would probably find, a much greater degree of public attention and admiration.

FINIS.

www.ingramcontent.com/pod-product-compliance
Lightning Source LLC
Chambersburg PA
CBHW020034030726
47499CB00007B/2427

* 9 7 8 3 3 3 7 3 9 7 4 4 9 *